GIRL
ON A HIGH
WIRE

GIRL
ON A HIGH
WIRE

Rae Foley

DODD, MEAD & COMPANY   *New York*

1 2 3 4 5 6 7 8 9 10

Library of Congress Catalog Card Number: 69-91277
ISBN 0-396-08163-0

*For the Old Mill
and the People Who Live There*

GIRL
ON A HIGH
WIRE

1

If it is true that coming events cast their shadows before, that morning should have started with a cyclone or an earthquake. Instead, it began exactly as five mornings a week had begun for the past two years.

I unlocked the door of the library, left it open for a few minutes to clear out the stale air, switched on lights, hung up my coat, turned over the calendar on the desk, revealing another blank page, changed the date on my stamp, and I was ready for business. This meant a thin trickle of women, mostly elderly, coming to select "a nice romance with a happy ending," and after school a too-brief stampede of youngsters.

The chief difference this morning was that, a week ago, I had come to a momentous decision. The library was about as varied and exciting as a treadmill. There were only three marriageable men of my age group in that small Pennsylvania town, and I had refused them all. The calendar with its blank page was a faithful picture of my life. So I had put an ad in the paper:

YOUNG WOMAN, twenty-three, good health, good disposition, driver's license, equipped to do secretarial work and simple home nursing, would like position as traveling companion for older woman. Call Catherine Briggs.

I had given the library telephone number for working hours and the one at my boarding house for evenings. Not that I actually expected anything to come of it. To the best of my knowledge, there wasn't an older woman in town who had either the means or the inclination to travel. I thought I would give it a week and then decide on my next move. All I was sure of was that there would be a move.

The telephone rang and a man's somewhat high-pitched voice said, "Miss Briggs?"

"This is Miss Briggs speaking."

"My name is Mitchell. The Mitchell Enterprises at Sixty-eight Main Street."

"Yes?"

"I saw your ad in the morning paper. Or rather my mother saw it. She is planning a trip abroad and, as she has never traveled, she would prefer to have someone with her to handle details, make reservations, deal with foreign currency, and all that. She doesn't need nursing, thank heaven, but she would like to have someone who could play two-handed card games or read aloud to her now and then. I'd prefer to talk it over with you and explain about my mother before you see her and find out if you'd—uh—be suitable."

I hadn't really expected it would happen. "Why, of course."

"Can you get away from the library for an hour or so? I'd like to set things up as quickly as possible and there would be a certain delay, anyhow, while you get your passport and all that. Is there anyone to replace you at the library so you can be here at my office at ten-thirty sharp?"

"I can't get a replacement, but I can close up and put a sign on the door."

2

"Fine. Be as prompt as you can, Miss Briggs. I have a busy schedule today."

"I'll be there at exactly ten-thirty."

As a kind of gesture I scrawled the appointment on the blank page of my calendar, though I was unlikely to forget the only event in an otherwise empty day. I had twenty minutes in which to make the five-minute walk, so there was no hurry. I wrote out a sign, CLOSED UNTIL TWELVE-THIRTY, and looked up as someone came into the library. Except for retired people, there were few men who ever entered the place. This one was heavy-set, with broken veins over his cheekbones and the kind of beard that looked dark unless he shaved twice a day. I didn't particularly care for the way he stared at me.

"You are Catherine Briggs?" Again that slow, searching look that took me in from head to foot. He even glanced, quite blatantly, at the jotting on the calendar. He raised his brows. "A new job prospect?"

"Well, really—"

He put up a stubby hand to check my indignant protest. "I'm a friend of Mrs. Harcourt, your aunt. She asked me to look you up when I came here. I got to town this morning and saw your ad in the paper while I was having breakfast at the Curtis House. Thought it must be the same Briggs girl."

I pushed back my chair. "Sorry. I have an appointment."

"Just a minute."

"And I don't believe you know my Aunt Geraldine. Now please go. I'll have to close the library temporarily."

He waited while I switched out lights, locked up, and thumbtacked the sign on the door. He had a hard

3

face and a common accent. He was about as different as it was possible to be from the kind of people Aunt Geraldine was likely to know. Men had tried in various ways to scrape up an acquaintance with me, but this was a new approach.

I went swiftly down the library steps, aware that after a moment's hesitation he had fallen in behind me. I stopped at a store window to study my reflection anxiously, dismayed to realize that last year's fall suit was the wrong length for fashion, and that my blouse was shabby. I hadn't owned a hat in several years, and I wondered if a hat would be expected. Mitchell Enterprises, according to a big announcement in the morning paper, was a Philadelphia outfit that was following the trend of moving out to smaller communities. Probably my clothes would look countrified to a city man. Then I noticed a hole in the finger of a glove, went into the store to buy white gloves, and waited impatiently for my change.

The morning was crisp and clear, one of those miraculous days that occur now and then in late October before the monotonous grayness of November, with the sky a cobalt blue and the air glistening, crisp and cool in the shade, almost hot in the sun.

I took a quick look around, but the man from the library was not lurking anywhere. The number I was seeking was in a building that had just been erected on Main Street. There was a scaffolding at the second-floor level where workmen were putting up a sign over a new shop. I was walking along a temporary boardwalk under the sign when there was a shout, something struck me between the shoulders, and I shot forward as though propelled out of a cannon and came dizzily to a stop against a wooden pile, while a crash

4

shook the boardwalk and re-echoed through the narrow passage.

Behind me a white-faced boy kept saying, "Jeez! Jeez!" There was wonder and horror and a kind of jubilation in his voice. I had, literally, grazed death by inches, by seconds. If it had not been for that powerfully built and beautifully co-ordinated boy shoving me out of the way, I would have been pulverized.

People gathered, as they do everywhere at the first indication of an accident, seeming to come out of the air, out of cracks. Someone steered me into the drugstore and onto a stool at the soda fountain, where the druggist brought me a smoky and unpleasant drink in a paper cup. At least it cleared my head and enabled me to assure people I hadn't been hurt, just rather horribly frightened by that brush with death—that quite accidental brush with death.

As a result of all this, I was late for my appointment at the office of Mitchell Enterprises, but that didn't matter, after all. Mr. Mitchell, whose deep voice was unlike the one on the telephone, had never heard of me. He had not asked me to call at his office. His mother had been dead for several years.

Even then there was no association in my mind between the fake telephone call and my near accident. It just seemed to be one of those days when I should have stayed in bed.

Before returning to the library, I decided to have an early lunch at the cafeteria. I wasn't really hungry, but I didn't want to have to close the library for a second time, so I got coffee and a paper-wrapped ham sandwich and set them on an unoccupied table. At the steam counter I saw a bulky figure and, as the man moved his tray along, I recognized him as the one who

5

had come into the library and tried to scrape up an acquaintance, claiming to be a friend of Aunt Geraldine.

I had forgotten mustard for the sandwich and went back for some. The man with the dark beard hesitated beside my chair and then went on to sit at a nearby table. On my way back to my own table, I encountered the nurse who had helped my father through his last illness, and we chatted a little while. All in all, perhaps five minutes passed before I returned with the mustard.

When I had first entered the cafeteria, I noticed a woman who was, quite frankly, scavenging food people had left at their tables. She picked up the remains of a sandwich and I wondered why on earth she stole scraps of food when there were so many places where she would be adequately fed without cost. As I approached my table, I saw her set down the coffee cup and hastily walk away. I pulled out my chair, reminding myself not to drink out of the cup. Then there was a crash, someone screamed, and I saw the woman lying on her face on the floor.

Someone bent over and then shouted in a panic, "She's dead!"

I pushed aside my untouched sandwich and left the cafeteria, unable to eat. Death seemed to have stalked me that morning, what with the falling sign that had so nearly struck me and a woman dying of heart failure practically at my table.

When I had opened the library again, I sat staring at the calendar on which I had noted the appointment with Mr. Mitchell. For the first time I wondered about that call. If it had been a joke, it had been a pointless one; it might, considering the falling sign, have been a fatal one.

Not until I heard the six o'clock news did I begin to be frightened for myself. An unidentified woman had fallen dead in a local cafeteria. Her death had been assumed to result from heart failure until an autopsy revealed that she had been poisoned by cyanide. Accident? Suicide? Murder? It seemed to be anyone's guess. Would witnesses to the incident please report to the police?

The local newscaster went on to say briskly, "A bizarre near-tragedy occurred this morning when a large sign being erected over the new branch of the Paris Shops on Main Street fell, nearly killing a woman pedestrian below. According to the workmen, a stranger joined them a few minutes prior to the accident, presumably sent by the management to help, let the sign slip out of his hands and, during the confusion that followed, disappeared. The management knows nothing of such a man. The police are investigating to learn his identity. Mental institutions in the vicinity report no patients unaccounted for."

That was when I faced the possibility that, twice in the day, someone had deliberately attempted to kill me. I didn't know why. There was no possible reason why. I was no threat to anyone. I had, so far as I knew, no enemies. There was nothing to be gained from a girl who had only her salary as a small-town librarian. Then why? All I could think of was the man with the dark beard, and he did not explain the puzzle—he merely intensified it.

I bit my nails and wondered what to do. To call the police and suggest that some unknown person wanted to kill me for an unknown reason was not apt to arouse any response beyond a conviction that I was unhinged. I was still worrying, still undecided, when there was an announcement on the eight o'clock news that funeral services were to be held day after tomorrow at eleven o'clock for Geraldine Forbes Harcourt, famous beauty, actress, social leader, and art patron. They were to be strictly private.

Not Aunt Geraldine! Not all that loveliness and vitality ended. And I had not even been informed of her death. True, I had played bridge with friends the night before and had not listened to the news, but someone should have told me.

According to the newscaster, the death had resulted from a fall on the spectacular staircase that was one of the architectural features of the famous Old Mill she had restored and made one of the beauty spots of New England. She had been dead for more than thirty-six hours when her body was found. Because of a breakdown in the heating system of the mill, all the occupants had been away, staying at a local motel until the furnace could be repaired. No one knew why Mrs. Harcourt had returned, unless she intended to check on the progress of the work.

Violent death, the voice went on cheerfully, seemed to dog the Old Mill, which had been the site of the savage Maybury killing some twenty years ago. Only two years before, the wife of a local man had been found drowned in the millstream. Until Mrs. Harcourt had decided to renovate the place, it had been regarded by some people as being haunted, because of odd lights and shadows that appeared from time to time.

I listened numbly to the broadcast. What hurt me most, somehow, was that Aunt Geraldine, who had loved people and had been so deeply loved in return, should have died alone.

Geraldine Forbes had always been news. She was news as an actress at eighteen because of her beauty, her talent, and her enormous vitality. More than one famous playwright had created a role especially for her.

She was news when, at twenty-six, she abandoned a spectacularly successful career on the stage to marry Gerald Harcourt, the steel magnate. The Man Who Always Knows assured everyone that she would be back on the stage within a year, that life with a much older man whose only interests outside of his huge business empire were in sports would bore her. But he was wrong. She never returned to the stage and she was never bored. She took her place in the society of New York and Southampton, of Palm Beach and Paris, as though she had been born to it.

She was news when, at fifty, she was left a wealthy widow. She withdrew from society as completely as she had withdrawn from the stage, bought the famous Old Mill that is always appearing on New England calendars, and restored it. Again The Man Who Always Knows was convinced that it would not last; the beautiful Mrs. Harcourt would never be happy in seclusion. Again he was proved wrong. Her interests, instead of retracting, seemed to expand and deepen and intensify.

And now, at sixty, she was news because she had fallen down her famous staircase at the Old Mill, breaking her neck and leaving a will whose provisions were to raise hell, cause horror, and bring violent death in their wake.

To me Geraldine Forbes Harcourt was little more than a name and a radiant dream. She had stopped acting before I was born and, because she had never appeared in movies, my only impression of her as a young woman was derived from a painting that hung in my father's study beside the portrait of my mother.

The sisters were incredibly alike and unmistakably different. They had the same small straight noses, the same wide-spaced dark eyes under heavy lids, the same curly hair like a soft dark cloud, and the same mouths with full lips tucked in at the corners. But my mother's portrait was like a faded reproduction of Aunt Geraldine's. The fires in her had never kindled, just smoldered and gone out, while they had blazed in her older sister.

My mother had been the last to marry, accepting a shy and serious young Latin teacher in the local high school. Though there had never been a break between the sisters, the paths they had followed were so different that they rarely crossed. In fact, I had seen Aunt Geraldine only three times: once when I was about eight and she came to spend a week with us, a glowing vision in wonderful furs, bearing beautiful gifts, and charging the very air with excitement. I adored her madly.

The second time was when I was fifteen. She stayed only for a weekend, and, though she wrought her incomparable magic, I was aware of a kind of unbridgeable gulf between the sisters. They no longer had anything to talk about. There was almost a quarrel when Aunt Geraldine offered to pay my college tuition.

"Her father and I feel," Mother said stiffly, "that if Cathy is not intelligent enough to merit a scholarship, she should not take the place of a more deserving student."

The last meeting was at my mother's funeral, two years ago, when Aunt Geraldine remained only a few hours between planes. Grieved as I was over Mother's death, which had followed a long illness, I was more shocked to see that Aunt Geraldine had, almost unfairly, retained much of her beauty, while my mother

10

for years had been faded and drab. This was the only time Aunt Geraldine really talked to me as though I were an adult. She asked what I planned to do, and I said I'd keep my job at the library of that small Pennsylvania town as long as my father needed me. He had been completely dependent on my mother and he couldn't manage by himself.

"Nonsense. A man like Henry always finds a woman willing and eager to look after him," Aunt Geraldine assured me. "Haven't you ever noticed the appeal of the helpless male to certain types of women?"

As I was about to protest at this slur on my father, she stopped me with a quick characteristic gesture of her hand, half imperative, half appealing, wholly irresistible. "Anyhow, you'll marry soon and your father will have to find another woman to cosset him. For all his retiring nature, it would never suit him to play second fiddle. You're bound to marry, you know, because you are so like me."

She turned me around to face the mirror and then stepped back, shielding her face. "No! No former beauty can contemplate old age philosophically when beside a current beauty. But just look at that portrait of me at twenty; it might be you, Cathy."

Seeing my genuine surprise, she laughed a little, pressing her fragrant cheek against mine. "Have you been brought up to think that your looks don't matter—only your fine character? Don't believe it. You are my younger self, with the same thirst for living. You mustn't try to pretend it isn't there or you'll stifle half yourself. I've envied Millie all these years for having you. But now it's my turn. Come see me, Cathy. Don't wait too long. Somehow life seems to slip away."

After that brief visit I never saw her again, but she

began to write warm, affectionate letters, revealing vivid glimpses of her life—the Old Mill she had restored and loved; the strange and amusing people she had collected around her: painters and writers and composers. Reading the letters in the dim library, looking along the dusty stacks, her words seemed to me to quiver with the real life of which this was a pallid reflection. I felt like the Lady of Shalott, seeing life only in a mirror.

But even when my father died, as quietly and unassumingly as he did everything, of a coronary, I did not suggest visiting Aunt Geraldine. There were two reasons. One was my awareness that my mother, whether from some unacknowledged jealousy or not, had been reluctant to let me visit her wealthy sister. The other was that Aunt Geraldine wrote, in amusement mixed with exasperation, to say that poor relations had descended on her like a plague of locusts, driving away her more interesting friends. I did not particularly care to add to the number of locusts.

"I do abominate family dissension," she wrote. "I always hated the Orestes trilogy. Hatred and vengeance that go on and on and on. It's so horribly destructive. Anything, anything for a quiet life. Anyhow, it is time to patch up all the old grievances, whether they are real or imaginary. And money, I notice—but I hope without cynicism—makes a serviceable and highly acceptable patch."

Her last two letters were different in tone from any I had ever had from her, lacking in her usual zest for living and her amusement at what went on around her. In one of them she said, "I have never been a nervous woman. It's the shadows that disturb me. Perhaps I need stronger glasses."

In the last letter, her very handwriting had changed,

sprawling so tall on the page that it was hard to make out the words, which stretched up like masts, running into those on the lines above.

"I do *not* imagine things or suffer from delusions. To attempt to prove that I do is monstrous. I am not a meek or a long-suffering woman, and so they will find out. I am taking steps today to end this intolerable situation."

I was putting the letter back in its envelope after rereading it when I noticed the postscript scrawled on the back of the last page: "When do you have your vacation? New England is breathtaking in October. Don't you want to see my beautiful mill? I want you to like it."

Even if I had understood that the words were an appeal to me, a cry for help, it would have been too late.

2

I was still trying to absorb the fact that anyone as vibrantly alive as Aunt Geraldine could just have been snuffed out like a candle, when my landlady called from the foot of the stairs, "Miss Briggs! Telegram for you."

The telephone was in the main hall, a chief source of entertainment and a springboard for conversation to the women who spent their lonely evenings in the parlor doing jigsaw puzzles, knitting, watching television, and occasionally playing bridge.

"'Funeral services for Mrs. Harcourt will be held here on Wednesday at eleven. Episcopal church. Please come if at all possible. Urgent.' The telegram," said an impersonal voice, "is signed Kendrick Knight."

Who Kendrick Knight was I had no idea, but he seemed determined that I should attend Aunt Geraldine's funeral. Anyhow, I was the only blood relation she had in the world. Someone of hers should be there to bid her that last farewell, not just "the plague of locusts" who had so annoyed her and, probably, exploited her.

As it was late in the month, my checking account was too low to enable me to travel by plane. I had to settle for a bus, though I did not look forward to a twelve-hour bus ride, which would get me into New York at midnight and would mean sitting on a bench in a bleak waiting room all night or entail the extra expense of a hotel until morning, when I could pick up another bus for Vermont.

The rain was almost of cloudburst proportions when I caught the bus for New York next day, and it was so dark, even at noon, that cars were using their dimmers. I hadn't slept much, what with frantic packing, pressing my one black dress, and borrowing a suitcase. There had been no time to think of anything beyond my immediate problems: finding a friend who could cash a check for me, canceling a date to play bridge, and arranging to close the library.

I took a last look around my room, went back on impulse to stuff letters, receipted bills, and canceled checks from my desk into my handbag. My landlady wasn't above snooping, and I didn't like having my personal affairs provide ammunition for an evening's gossip. It's just as well I didn't guess how much ammunition I was going to provide.

With my coat collar turned up as a protection from the driving rain, I collected the suitcase and my handbag. I didn't own an umbrella and I rarely wore a rainhood, as my hair, thank heaven, is naturally curly, which saves a fortune in beauty parlors.

The postman was leaving mail on the hall table when I went down. There was nothing for me but a rolled newspaper, which I tucked under my arm for something to read on the bus.

When I had settled in my seat, I stared at the streaming window, but it was impossible to see anything outside, so I opened the newspaper. The sight of Aunt Geraldine's familiar writing jolted me. Across the top of the first page she had scrawled, "It *is* a nice idea,

15

isn't it? More fun than the library? What do you think? Come and see for yourself."

There was a heart-lifting moment when I thought the account of her death had been some gigantic blunder. Then I noticed the date of the cancellation stamp. The paper had been mailed some days earlier. It was an unpretentious local weekly, an eight-page affair, owned and edited by Kendrick Knight. This answered one question, the identity of the man who had sent me that urgent telegram.

The story was featured on page one:

A MACDOWELL COLONY FOR MILLTOWN

Mrs. Gerald Harcourt, who acquired the Old Mill ten years ago, and has since transformed it into one of New England's beauty spots, has announced her plan to build cottages in the woods attached to the mill grounds—there are five thousand acres—and provide facilities for composers, painters, and writers. Since an artists' colony in California was closed for lack of funds several years ago, there are too few places where the young creative artist can work at his own tempo, without interruption or financial worry, Mrs. Harcourt said today.

Geraldine Forbes Harcourt has been known to the American public all her life. Her rare beauty has long attracted painters and sculptors for whom she has sat. As Geraldine Forbes, she was regarded as one of the most brilliant actresses on Broadway. As the wife of the prominent industrialist and sportsman, Gerald Harcourt, she became a famous and popular leader in society, not only in New York but among the International Set. In her widowhood, this gracious and lovely woman has continued to create around her a world of beauty.

Long abandoned, the Old Mill was a local eyesore. Because several sudden deaths had occurred on the premises, the place was feared and avoided by the people of Milltown. Today, it is one of New England's glories. The natural beauty of the grounds remains unspoiled, as does the millstream. The great living room with its magnificent hanging staircase (pictures on page three) is arrestingly beautiful though comparatively unknown, as Mrs. Harcourt is averse to intrusion on her privacy.

This morning, Mrs. Harcourt announced her intention of making the grounds of the Old Mill a refuge for artists, though she rejects with indignation and distaste the role of Lady Bountiful or patroness. "I am the one to be most gratified if talented people can find here the peace in which to work," she told this reporter. "The company of creative people is stimulating and exciting."

"Some sort of foundation, I suppose, must be set up to administer the place, handle the financing, and select the artists. It is not an original idea, of course. Mrs. Edward MacDowell deserves the full credit for that. But I think it is a nice one, don't you?"

This reporter, kindled by her excitement and enthusiasm, agreed wholeheartedly.

That man had been in love with Aunt Geraldine, I thought. Then I turned to page three and saw the pictures. There was a reproduction of a painting of Aunt

Geraldine done some thirty years ago by a famous artist. It was a face for which men would have sacked cities, if that had been what she wanted.

There was a candid camera shot, taken recently, squinting a little as she looked into the light, and smiling. I remembered the smile. It was irresistible. Even the white hair had not faded her. Even in brilliant sunlight she was still lovely, though her body had thickened and the skin had slackened along the jawline, and there were wrinkles at the corners of her eyes and lips.

The third picture was an interior shot of the great living room of the mill, focused chiefly on the staircase—the staircase, I remembered, down which Aunt Geraldine had plunged to her death. It had been built out into the room, with a few low steps of what appeared to be white stone with slender iron railings leading to a broad landing beyond which I could see a window that extended to the roof of the building. Above the landing, winding out over the center of the room, the stairs soared upward in a lovely curving line like a circular staircase.

I tore out the news story and the pictures and stuffed them into my handbag, making it bulge so I had to struggle to fasten it. The bus rocketed along, spraying muddy water on the windshields of smaller cars. I couldn't sleep. I thought of the fake telephone call that had taken me under the sign just as the unknown man had let it drop. I thought of the man who had paused beside my table in the cafeteria and of the poor woman who had died, poisoned, after drinking from my coffee cup. And finally I thought of the telegram from Kendrick Knight, asking me to come to the funeral. Urgent, he had said. Urgent.

The bus came to a grinding stop. I couldn't see through the curtain of rain, but a rumor soon spread that the bridge ahead had been washed out and we would have to be rerouted. A passenger who had a seat on a flight for London from Kennedy Airport set up a howl, his rage and frustration falling on the defenseless head of the driver who, of course, was not to blame for the weather.

I had been dozing uneasily for several hours, rousing with a start when, in some unidentified small town, an ambulance screamed past, roof light blinking; or when, in the seat ahead, a sleeping man uttered a loud snore. But we all awakened when there was a report almost like that of a shotgun. The driver pulled over to the side of the road, hazard lights blinking, and I heard him speak into a small two-way radio, heard a metallic voice reply. Then he stood up, straightened tired shoulders, and looked at us, half apologetically, half defensively.

"Sorry, folks. You'll have to wait here for a while. There is some mechanical trouble."

"You mean you can't drive it as it is?"

The driver shrugged. "Not unless you want to ride in a bus without brakes or low gear. The company will send another bus to pick you up."

The man whose flight was now definitely out of the question threatened not only to report the driver's inefficiency but to give the whole disgraceful situation a public airing.

"You do that," the driver said amiably.

Even the grumblers were asleep when the replacement bus arrived. We stumbled from one to the other. I was dimly aware that the temperature had dropped since I left home. Through sleep-filled eyes I peered at my watch. Three o'clock in the morning. Zero hour. I was asleep again almost as soon as I got into my seat.

Because of the unforeseen delays, it was morning

19

when I was awakened by a general stirring of the passengers. I looked to the east and caught one overwhelming view of midtown New York, a vast incredible mountain of steel and glass, before the bus started up a steep curving ramp. The uneasy imaginings of the night were gone. This was New York and I was excited as though the curtain was about to go up on a play.

In the enormous Port Authority Bus Terminal there was just time for coffee and doughnuts at a stand before the bus for Vermont pulled out. I was going to be late for the funeral. Actually, I was an hour too late. It was twelve o'clock when the bus stopped at Milltown. I went into the little one-room office that served as a combination bus station, headquarters for the local taxi, Western Union, and real-estate office.

A thin man wearing red suspenders, a green eyeshade pushed up on his forehead, was typing in two-fingered fashion at a machine, *circa* 1905. He looked at me and pushed back his chair.

"You'll be Mrs. Harcourt's niece. I could have picked you out of a million. Like as two peas. I always thought it would have been something to know her forty years ago. You're late for the funeral."

I explained about the cloudburst and the bridge that had been washed out and the breakdown of the bus because of some mysterious mechanical ailment.

"Don't let it worry you," the man said unexpectedly. "Mrs. Harcourt didn't hold by all these services. Simple is the way she wanted it. No flowers. No eulogies. No fuss. Well, they didn't pay attention. Parading their grief." He snorted.

"They?"

"Bunch of no-count relations." The man added hastily, "Mr. Harcourt's family. Not hers."

"Where can I get a taxi?"

"You can't. There's only one and it took a load of people to the funeral. Anyhow, you can walk to the mill easy. Leave your suitcase here; it will be safe enough. That all you brought?"

I nodded.

"People mostly come to the Old Mill prepared to dig in. Permanent. I wouldn't care for it myself. Queer things have happened there. Anyhow, you can't miss it. It's a dead-end road. Down Main Street to the blinker. Turn left, maybe a quarter of a mile. The mill-stream will be on your right. Follow it to a rustic bridge. The house is across the bridge and the key to the side door is in a big Chinese sort of vase on the porch."

I laughed. "Aunt Geraldine must have been a very trusting person."

"Yeah." He peered at me over his glasses. "Kind of a shame, isn't it?" Having made his point, he picked up the suitcase and hoisted it onto a shelf. He had said all he intended to say.

Milltown is not a picturesque New England village. As far as I could make out, as I walked quickly along Main Street, it had been settled in the late 1700s or early 1800s by small manufacturers, had achieved its peak of affluence about 1880, and then had gone into a decline—not a mellow and romantic decline, but a sort of rot.

As individual manufacturers had been absorbed by larger ones, the original settlers had moved away, leaving behind their decaying buildings with broken windows. It was like a one-company town after a six-month strike. There were a few stately houses on Main Street, two white Colonials and a handsome Georgian structure, but on the whole the houses were small, rundown, with peeling paint and overgrown gardens. There was one block of split-level houses, exactly alike except for the paint jobs, and with no gardens at all. But this sporadic burst into the twentieth century had stopped short there.

When I turned left at the blinker, I began to find the New England I was seeking. The great trees still bore a few red and crimson and gold leaves, the ground was a scarlet carpet, which crackled as I scuffled through it. Unexpectedly the sun came out, and the sky, leaden and lowering for eighteen hours, was a deep brilliant blue. It should have been a good omen.

I crossed the road and followed the millstream, which ran briskly and noisily over stones. Beyond, I could see the mill itself. I had not been prepared for its size. I paused on the rustic bridge, looking at the grounds, at the grandeur of arching elms that met over a curving driveway on the opposite side of the house, at a new addition on the north, at the cutting garden still bright with late flowers, and beyond into the woods.

By coming on foot I had approached the house from the back. At the side there was a deep screened porch. I opened the screened door and stood hesitating. There was no sound in the house. Apparently everyone had gone to the funeral.

Feeling like an intruder, I groped in a great cloisonné jar that should have been in a museum and found the key. The door opened onto a dining room, and beyond that was the living room of the mill, which was much larger than I had expected and was, by all odds, the most delightful room I had ever seen, with deep windows on three sides, and unexpected nooks and corners. On the north, a baby grand piano seemed almost lost, silhouetted against a window with a wide cushioned seat. On the east was the front door, on either side casement windows, a love seat, deep chairs, and tables.

On the west side a great stone fireplace had been built out from the wall, and behind it was another table with a bowl of chrysanthemums that were beginning to wilt. The staircase was, of course, the dominating feature and, between it and the fireplace, in a space larger than most living rooms, were grouped couches, half a dozen chairs, more tables and lamps.

Big and sprawling as the room was, it had maintained a curious atmosphere of intimacy; it gave the impression of being lived in. There was none of the rigidity of the decorated room. But the housekeeping had been slack, or perhaps that was because of Aunt Geraldine's sudden death. Ashtrays had not been emptied, a wastebasket was filled to overflowing, and a magazine had been left open on a table.

As something moved at the edge of my vision, I whirled around, my heart thumping, but I was alone. In spite of the number and size of the windows, the room seemed dark and I realized that the sun had gone behind a cloud again. I found myself looking over my shoulder. Just a shadow. The room was filled with shadows. Aunt Geraldine had spoken of shadows.

I didn't care to go upstairs, not knowing which room I was expected to occupy; if, indeed, I was expected to stay overnight at the mill. After all, the request for me to come had not emanated from the people who lived here; they had not even bothered to inform me of Aunt Geraldine's death. But if I could not stay here, I would have to cash a check somewhere. Perhaps I could ask the newspaper owner, who seemed to love Aunt Geraldine and who had urged me so insistently to attend her funeral, whether he would vouch for me.

The house felt chilly. The ashes in the fireplace were cold, and I couldn't find a thermostat to turn up the furnace heat. I had a curious feeling that I was not alone in the room. All of a sudden I wanted, like the starling, to get out. I turned up my coat collar and went out on the side porch, walking away from the mill so that I could get a better impression of it as a whole from a distance. At least that is what I told myself. Actually, it was a relief to be outside.

Then the sun emerged again and set the chuckling water in the millstream to sparkling like a southern night sky filled with stars. Slowly I began to follow the stream. The water was so clear that I could see the stones on the bottom, see an old shoe, see—

The shoe moved as I looked at it, moved to the right, to the left. It could move only a few inches either way. The man's leg seemed to be wedged under an over-hanging rock. He made no attempt to release it. He lay on his face.

I found myself shouting, but there was no one to hear me. I didn't dare waste time hunting for a telephone. He might still be alive.

I flung myself full length on the ground beside the stream and tried to reach him. Cautiously I worked my way to the very edge, stretching out my arms, leaning over until I nearly overbalanced and toppled into the water. My fingers touched cloth and slipped on it. I couldn't get a grip on the coat. I grabbed his hair, but it was too short to hold. Then I got both hands under his chin and tried to lift his head out of the water.

"What the hell," a voice behind me exclaimed, "do you think you are doing?"

I didn't dare move for fear I'd lose my grip on that chin. "There's someone in the millstream. I can't get him out."

I was shoved unceremoniously aside and then there was a splash as a man dropped into the stream, steadying himself against the rush and the shock of the cold water. He bent over and freed the wedged leg. Then he heaved the fellow over on his back. Open eyes stared up sightlessly through the water.

"Is he dead?" I asked stupidly.

"Very." The voice was dry. Then, as I turned to scramble to my feet, he saw my face. "Good God!" He slipped on a stone, hauled himself up on the bank, his dark slacks streaming water. He wore a dark gray sweater and a thick plaid woodsman's jacket. He held out his hand and pulled me to my feet. "Here, you aren't going to faint, are you?"

I shook my head.

"Then we had better get to a phone and call the police."

I hung back. "Are you just going to leave him there?"

"We'll have to leave him until the police see him." As I made a little sound of distress, he added reasonably, "It won't matter to him now, you know." He propelled me into the house. The telephone was on the table behind the fireplace with the bowl of chrysanthemums. The man went toward it without hesitation, so I took for granted that he was one of the poor relations. At least he knew his way around the house. He picked up the telephone and then set it back in its cradle, looking at me with narrowed eyes. "How did you happen to find him?"

"I just got here. I am—"

"I know who you must be. Catherine Briggs. You look so much like your aunt it knocked me for a loop. You didn't go to the funeral."

I explained about the series of accidents that had

delayed the bus. He nodded, checking off points. "Good. Then Bailey can testify you came in on the bus at twelve o'clock." As I started to speak, he forestalled me impatiently. "Bailey. Guy at the bus station."

"Why, yes. I left my suitcase there. Only what difference—"

"That man in the millstream didn't lie down there and go to sleep, Miss Briggs. You realize that?"

"Of course not, but," I gaped at him, "by any possible chance, do you think I killed him?"

"Someone did. Someone sure as hell did. There's a lump behind his left ear."

I sat down limply.

"But if you are in the clear," he reached for the telephone, "never saw the guy before—"

"I didn't say that. I saw him day before yesterday in Pennsylvania and I think he tried twice to kill me. Only I don't know why."

3

He was a thin-faced man of about thirty, of medium height, with a casual air, narrow eyes, and nothing particularly arresting in his appearance. He shoved aside the telephone, groped in his pocket, and said "Damn!"

"There are cigarettes on the table."

"I've stopped smoking," he snapped, and in spite of my state of shock, I found myself grinning.

"How long? Two days?"

"Two weeks. Sorry. It keeps me edgy. That and other things. Oh, by the way, my name is Knight. Kendrick Knight. I publish the local weekly."

"Oh." I was taken aback and showed it.

"What's odd about that?"

"Just—I read the story you wrote about Aunt Geraldine and the mill and the art colony, and I got the idea somehow that you were a much older man and that you loved her."

"I did love her. She was a lovely person, Miss Briggs."

"But you didn't go to her funeral."

"You haven't seen the leeches she had around her. The sight of them pretending to mourn would have made me sick." He sounded savage. Then he groped absently for a cigarette and snapped his fingers. "Look here, we've got to talk fast before that—that—"

27

"Plague of locusts," I said helpfully. "That's what Aunt Geraldine called them."

"Did she?" For a moment his face warmed. "Now," and his voice was brisk, "tell me what you know about the dead man. Everything. And, for God's sake, be quick about it. We've got to call the police without further delay."

"What do you want to know?"

"Everything that has anything to do with the man."

I didn't question his right to ask, which surprised me when I thought about it later. I started meekly with the man's sudden appearance in the library. I repeated our brief conversation as accurately as possible. Then I backtracked to explain about the fake telephone call from Mr. Mitchell in answer to my advertisement and how the man in the library had seen my notation on the calendar.

"He said Aunt Geraldine had asked him to look me up."

"But you didn't believe him. Why?"

"He wasn't her kind of person, not a man she would ever have sent to me. He was common and tough and—I can't explain because it sounds exaggerated. Evil. The thing is, Mr. Knight—"

"I'm Kendrick. Ken's shorter. Your aunt called you Cathy, didn't she?"

I nodded.

"Well? Go on, Cathy."

So I told him about the near accident and the strange workman who had dropped the sign and disappeared. I told him about seeing the man from the library loiter beside my table in the cafeteria, and the woman who had drunk from my coffee cup and fallen dead. That night the newscaster said she had been poisoned with cyanide.

28

"God!" The syllable was jerked from between tight lips. "Did you call the police to report these attacks on you?"

I shook my head. "I didn't know what to do. It sounded—crazy. Really crazy, I mean. There's no reason why anyone should want to kill me."

"There's a reason," he said slowly, "though I don't know how anyone found out. You're in a spot, Cathy, and the hell of it is that I put you there. I can't explain the whole thing now. Wheels within wheels. But I suggest you keep still about ever having seen that man before. I don't want someone getting ideas." He leaned forward, caught my shoulders, and made me look at him. "You don't know this man," he said slowly and clearly. "You just got here. I'm the one who found him in the millstream. Don't get involved. Do you understand?"

"Aren't you getting yourself involved?"

"To the best of my belief, someone has already attempted to involve me. You'll be okay. Just think before you speak and don't volunteer anything." He looked at me uneasily. "Are you paying attention?"

"Yes."

Still with that worried look, he dialed a number. "This is Kendrick Knight, speaking from the Old Mill. I've found another body . . . I don't know who he is. Just turned him over to make sure he was not alive . . . In the millstream . . . I don't see how it could be an accident. There's a lump the size of an egg behind his left ear . . . Quite definitely murder, I'd say. Get Captain Grieg, will you? He knows . . . Well, it would be stretching coincidence, wouldn't it, if there should be two? . . . Good. Thank you."

When he had set down the telephone, I asked, "Two?"

29

"You might as well hear it from me, Cathy. I believe your aunt was murdered. I'm the one who found her, you know. That's why I came today, while everyone would be out. I wanted to see whether I could uncover anything, any trace—"

"Oh, no! Not Aunt Geraldine. She fell down the stairs."

"She plunged down from the second floor. She was found on the landing with a broken neck. But her body had been bruised when she banged from side to side on that circular staircase without attempting to protect herself."

I moistened dry lips. "You mean she was unconscious before she fell?"

"She must have been. Don't you remember the way she moved? As quick and light on her feet as a cat. She wasn't a person to lose her balance; she'd had so much training in the use of her body that it was instinctive, and she always kept herself supple and active."

"But why—she was so kind, so lovely, so generous. What do they say—the people who have been living here?".

"The people who have been living here say accident. Naturally they would. I haven't confided my opinion in anyone but Captain Grieg, and he doesn't confide in me."

"Wouldn't her doctor have known if something had been wrong?"

"Dr. Graves issued the death certificate without a moment's hesitation. As he is also medical examiner, there was no further question. Some natural tears he shed. That's about all."

Something in his voice made me look at him questioningly. "Surely you don't think a reputable physician would cover up a thing like murder. Certainly not a medical examiner!"

"Oh, Graves has a good reputation. The best. Greatly loved. The vanishing type of family doctor. General practitioner. How much medicine he knows I have no idea, but he has an impeccable bedside manner."

"You don't like him."

"I have nothing against him, but I would not want him prescribing for me. He probably orders physic for appendicitis. But Mrs. Harcourt," his voice warmed when he mentioned her, "liked him. Quite the old family friend."

The room seemed to be getting colder and colder. I got up stiffly and began to walk up and down. My coat was buttoned to the throat, my icy hands thrust deep in my pockets.

"Sorry, Mr. Knight," I said at last.

"Ken," he said absently.

"I can't do it your way. If Aunt Geraldine was murdered, the police ought to know all the facts. I'm not going to stand in their way. I'll help all I can."

"What you will probably accomplish by that noble attitude," he said glumly, "is to drag a nice red herring across the path, link yourself with the dead man, and cause all sorts of unnecessary trouble." He broke off. "You're cold. Why didn't you tell me?" He went into the dining room, there was a thin, clear ring of crystal, and he came back holding a fragile long-stemmed wine glass, which he thrust into my hand. "Sherry. I hope you like it dry. Drink it. All of it."

He found the thermostat and turned it up. Then he opened the fire screen, piled up white birch logs, thrust a Cape Cod lighter under them, and dropped in a lighted match. Fire licked along the logs while he sat back watching. Then he pulled a big chair close to the fire. "You'd better keep on your coat until the place is warmer."

I settled back in the chair and was comforted when the furnace came on with a thump. I didn't know what to make of him. He was as alien as it was possible to be from the standard concept of a village newspaperman. Everything about him was big-city, sophisticated, even important, in an understated way. And yet he dressed like a casual country man; he had none of the stigmata of the celebrity, he was completely unself-conscious. I suppose what came through was a kind of inner balance, made up of discipline and an awareness that he could cope with most situations in which he found himself. Another thing that came through, obviously and disturbingly, was that he had no faith at all that I could cope with the situation in which he thought I was involved, and that he felt responsible for me. I wasn't sure whether I was grateful or whether I resented his attitude.

A car door slammed and he took a long look at me, started to say something, and then went to open the front door. There was no vestibule and the door opened directly on the living room, so that a cold wind swirled around my ankles. Facing the fireplace in the big chair, I did not see the two men but I could hear them, a heavy voice with a slight Norwegian lilt, and a young voice that was lighter in pitch.

"You didn't waste much time, Grieg," Ken said. "Oh, you're Sergeant Mendelssohn, aren't you?"

"Yes, sir," said the young voice. "We can't help the comic effect of sounding like something in an orchestra instead of a police force."

"We were clearing a way for the funeral procession

32

on its way from the church to the cemetery," the deeper voice said. "You didn't attend the church services."

Ken did not bother to confirm the obvious.

"Desk man reported there is a body in the millstream. Murdered. That's what he thought you said."

"That's what I did say."

"Your mind seems to run to murder."

"I seem to encounter it." There was a touch of hostility in Ken's voice.

"When did you find this body? And how? And why were you here, anyhow, during the services for Mrs. Harcourt? I thought you were a special friend of hers."

There was something odd in the air. It occurred to me that the men from the state police barracks were almost hostile toward Kendrick Knight. Because he claimed to have found "another" body?

That settled it. I stood up. The two men stared at me, a square man in plain clothes, and a younger, thinner, taller man in the trim uniform of the state police.

"I'm the one who found him, not Mr. Knight. I am Mrs. Harcourt's niece, Catherine Briggs. I got here a few minutes ago, and—"

"Later," the captain suggested. His eyes rested speculatively on Ken's slacks, dripping water on the deep pile of the Persian rug. "Suppose you show us." As I started for the side door, he said hastily, "Not you, Miss Briggs. Knight knows the way." Again there was that odd undercurrent.

The three men went through the dining room. Only when the side door had closed did I hear their voices and then they were pitched so low I could barely make out the words of the young sergeant.

"My God, I thought I was seeing things! She's sure like Mrs. Harcourt."

I was warmer now and I slipped off my coat, walking aimlessly around the room, stopping to look at the staircase, to picture Aunt Geraldine hurtling down, bouncing helplessly from side to side. Murder. A familiar enough word, heaven knows, in a violent world, but one outside my experience. Or was it? There was a dead man in the millstream; a man who, twice, so I believed, had tried to kill me.

I was careful not to look out toward the stream at the activities of the three men as they stood on the bank. There had been something watchful in the eyes of the police as they studied Ken, something guarded in his manner. A queer kind of cat-and-mouse game they seemed to be playing.

I curled up in a corner of a couch near the fire, still holding the wine glass. And then I waited. It seemed like an eternity; it was probably less than five minutes before Captain Grieg came back with Ken. The latter was sneezing.

"Better get out of those wet clothes before you catch cold," the captain said.

"I'm not leaving."

"Then borrow some dry slacks. Isn't there a man here whose clothes would fit you?"

"Guthrie is too heavy and Maine is too tall, but perhaps I can manage." Obviously the newspaper editor did not want to leave me alone with the police captain, but after a moment he shrugged and ran up the stairs.

"Now, Miss Briggs," Captain Grieg said, "suppose you tell me about it." As I hesitated, wondering what was relevant, he added encouragingly, "I've got a daughter about your age. Twenty?"

34

"Twenty-three."

"No one would ever question your relationship to Mrs. Harcourt. Astonishing resemblance. Might be mother and daughter."

"My mother was her younger sister and they looked a lot alike, almost identical, though they weren't twins."

Captain Grieg seemed to be the fatherly type, a rather thick man with blond hair frosted with gray and a Scandinavian cast of feature. "Too bad you missed the funeral."

I explained about the series of accidents that had delayed the bus. "I couldn't afford to fly, but Mr. Knight's telegram seemed sort of—urgent, so I thought I had better come."

"Knight urged you to come to the funeral? Have you known him long?"

"I never saw him until just now."

"But you planned to meet him here."

I was so surprised that I blurted out, "Why on earth would I have done that? I meant to be in time for the services, but when I was so late and there was no transportation to the cemetery, I decided to come here to the mill."

"Now, Miss Briggs, tell me about finding that body. Must have been a bad shock, coming across a strange man dead like that."

I burned my bridges. All along I had known that I would have to. "I had seen him before." As I had already told the story to Ken Knight, it was easier a second time. Now and then, I looked doubtfully at Captain Grieg, but his face did not reveal what he thought. I jumped nervously when a siren sounded and he said in that soothing voice of his, "Just the squad boys coming to take pictures, get fingerprints, and all that. Routine. Sergeant Mendelssohn will soon be free to join us and take down your statement."

Kendrick Knight ran down the stairs, wearing beautifully tailored slacks of pale yellow that were too long for him, a blue shirt with a monogram on the pocket, and leather bedroom slippers that also had monograms.

Grieg took in this magnificence in one sardonic glance. "What the well-dressed man should wear. All you need is a chain around your neck."

"You go to—" Ken broke off and returned the grin. His narrow eyes narrowed still more when he smiled. As the sergeant came in and, after an inquiring glance at the captain, sat down and pulled out a notebook, Ken settled himself with the air of a man who intends to remain put.

"Do you," Grieg asked mildly, "represent Miss Briggs' interests?"

"I think it might be a good idea if someone did."

"I understood that you and she had just met."

"You didn't ask me how long I had known her." As though to escape the captain's steady scrutiny, Ken leaned forward to take a cigarette out of the jade box on the table, and then withdrew his empty hand and tapped nervously on the arm of his chair.

The captain was annoyed but he was also, I thought, troubled. Had he dismissed the idea of Aunt Geraldine having been murdered and then changed his mind when he saw the body in the millstream? I got the impression, somehow, that he was suspicious of Ken, that the body in the millstream had a meaning for both of them that it lacked for me, that they shared some knowledge.

Grieg turned to me with that fatherly smile of his.

"Now, Miss Briggs, you say the first time you saw that poor fellow," and he nodded his head in the direction of the millstream, "was when he appeared several days ago, in the library of your home town in Pennsylvania and told you that Mrs. Harcourt had suggested that he look you up."

Sergeant Mendelssohn's pen nearly ran off the page. Ken stopped his nervous tapping and shot me a quick, reproachful look. Then he shrugged in resignation.

"Suppose we just go over it again. Let the sergeant get down all your—extraordinary experiences with this man." The captain sounded as jovial as a teacher telling a kindergarten class about an unexpected treat.

So for the third time I went over the whole thing: the telephone call that was supposed to come from Mr. Mitchell, the man in the library who claimed to know my aunt, the falling sign and the stranger who had dropped it and disappeared, the woman who had died of cyanide poisoning after drinking from my coffee cup, and the man who had stopped at my table in the cafeteria just moments before.

"Of course you reported these—incidents—to your local police."

I shook my head. "It sounded so unlikely, the kind of thing a person with a persecution mania would imagine."

Captain Grieg did not dispute that.

"You see, I was still trying to decide what I ought to do when the whole thing was knocked out of my head by hearing of Aunt Geraldine's death. Then I got the telegram from Mr. Knight, asking me to come to the funeral, and after that I didn't have time for anything but preparing for the trip."

Grieg turned for a long look at Kendrick Knight. "You wanted Miss Briggs to come?"

37

"I thought she ought to be here. I hope I didn't make a mistake about that. If I did, the least I can do is to look out for her."

"You think she is going to need looking out for?"

"I think it is very likely. Someone isn't playing games, Captain. At least, the name of that game is murder."

4

Car doors slammed and there were voices. "Police cars! Three of them!" a woman exclaimed. "And that old Plymouth of Ken's. What on earth—"

The front door was flung open and a party of five people came in, a young woman and four men. The woman was tall and slim, with short blond hair swept up from her face. Even in a conventional black suit with a small black hat she was, in some intangible way, unconventional. She moved like an athlete, and she almost vibrated with energy. Her shoulders were broad for a woman. She was, I supposed, about thirty, with small features and clear blue eyes. At first glance, everything about her, from the tanned skin to the long swing of the leg from the hip as she walked, suggested the outdoor sort of person. At second glance, even to my inexperienced eyes, she was a woman on the prowl.

Her eyes moved swiftly from Grieg to Mendelssohn to Kendrick Knight. They stopped there. She wasn't a woman to notice another woman while there were men around.

"Ken darling! What's going on? The police—" She broke off, staring out through the dining room window toward the millstream. "What's happened?" Her voice was louder, almost shrill. Then, belatedly, she saw me. "My God! You must be—"

"You," intervened a pleasant voice, so smoothly that it was hardly an interruption, "must be Geraldine's niece." He was about sixty-five, with a round body and round face and round horn-rimmed glasses. He took my hand. "I am Geraldine's brother-in-law, Guthrie Harcourt." He squeezed my hand in an avuncular sort of way. "My daughter Nell and my son Maine."

Maine was like his sister in appearance, tall and blond and elegant. He wore his beautifully tailored clothes with a careless grace. He was, unfairly, better-looking than Nell; indeed, he could, without exaggeration, be called handsome. But he lacked her super-charged energy. There was an air of languor about him, but whether it was innate or cultivated, I did not know.

To my surprise, he kissed me lightly on the cheek. "A cousin's privilege," he declared.

"Cousin?" Nell challenged him.

Her father chuckled. "Well, it's all in the family, isn't it? And if Maine can resist a beautiful girl, I'll disown him."

Maine seemed to be only mildly interested in the presence of the police; he was more interested in Kendrick's attire, especially the monogram on shirt pocket and slippers. "Where did you get those clothes?"

"From your room. I took a dip in the millstream. I'll return the stuff to you tomorrow."

"No hurry. But what were you doing in the millstream?"

The fourth member of the party waited for Ken's answer and, when it was not forthcoming, he turned to me. "Miss Briggs, I am Arthur Mattheson, your aunt's attorney."

40

From the moment the funeral party had entered the room, I had been intensely conscious of him. To this day I don't know whether he was good-looking. I do know that, handsome as Maine was, no woman would be likely to notice him when the lawyer was around. He was in his middle thirties and the tallest of the men, with the exception of the slim young sergeant. His voice would have made an actor's fortune. In any group, I thought, people would without hesitation accept his right of leadership.

He looked at Ken with raised eyebrows. "Too bad you were unable to attend the services." His eyes flicked back to me. "Or perhaps not. You aren't a man to waste your time."

Ken gave him a lazy grin, but he made no comment. The hostility between the two men was like the flash and clash of crossing blades. But in the lawyer's face there was more than that; there was distrust and an awakening suspicion.

The last member of the party was a man of sixty, a man who, to judge by the lines in his face, usually wore a cheerful expression. Right now he was badly shaken. Of them all, he was the only one who appeared to have been genuinely moved by Aunt Geraldine's funeral. He stood staring at me, startled, and then he came to rest his hands lightly on my shoulders.

"So you are Geraldine's dear Cathy. You're so— incredibly like her." For a moment his voice was unsteady and then he smiled at me. Belatedly he seemed to be aware of the presence of the police, of the activities that were visible through the dining room window. "Has something happened?"

Captain Grieg took charge with quiet authority. "Sorry to have bad news for you, Dr. Graves. For all of you. We have just found," there was a small and, I think, intentional pause, "another body."

Guthrie Harcourt's jaw dropped. "Another—"

"A dead man in the millstream. It looks like murder. I'm sorry to have to ask you at such a time, when you have just returned from Mrs. Harcourt's funeral, but I want you to look at him, Doctor. As medical examiner you'd have to, sooner or later."

"Of course."

"In fact, I would like all of you to look at him."

"Why?" The geniality was wiped off Guthrie's round face.

Maine touched his father's arm. There was a gray line around his mouth, but his voice was quiet; it almost seemed to carry a note of warning. "Of course. A natural thing to ask."

Guthrie shook off his son's hand. "But what have I to do with it?" If Maine's color had faded, his father's had deepened; even his bald head was scarlet.

"The road to the mill is a dead end," Grieg pointed out. "The man must have been coming here, so the chances are that he knew Mrs. Harcourt, that some of you might have seen him before."

For a moment I thought Guthrie was going to refuse. Then Maine took his arm and the two men followed Dr. Graves out of the room.

The lawyer looked from Ken to me. "I take it that Miss Briggs and Knight have already viewed the body."

"That's right," Grieg said.

Mattheson gave Ken a sharp, troubled look. Then he smiled at me in reassurance and followed the other men out to the millstream.

As though she had been waiting for this moment, Nell went to slip her hand under Ken's arm in a possessive gesture. "Come with me, darling, and hold my hand. It's too grim."

He released himself casually. "Better get it over," he advised her.

Somewhere a door opened and closed. There were muted voices. The captain went through the dining room and opened a swinging door onto a gleaming, modern kitchen.

"Please come this way."

A stocky young man, the kind who appears to be middle-aged before he is twenty, and a skinny girl, sloppily dressed, her untidy hair in a pony tail tied with a black ribbon, came into the room, looking as wary as undomesticated animals as they obeyed the official summons.

"This is Mrs. Harcourt's couple," Ken told me. "Leopold and Sonia Wenski. Wenski is preparing to make his debut as a concert pianist, and your aunt built on that studio room to provide him with a place in which he can practice."

Nell took a cigarette out of the box and waited for Ken to light it. "What took you so long?"

The houseman had an unexpectedly deep and resonant voice with a midwestern accent that did not fit his name. "Not having a car and not being offered a lift," he said in so surly a manner that I was startled, "we had to walk back from the cemetery."

"Oh, well, as long as you are here, get lunch right away, but first bring us some drinks, for God's sake! There's something about funerals—"

Sonia Wenski did not seem to be the kind of cook Aunt Geraldine would employ. There was an unwashed air about her and she stood taking unpleasantly furtive looks around her. As she caught sight of me, her eyes widened, went back to the police. When

43

she spoke, her voice, like her manner, was tinged with impertinence. "I don't know who is supposed to give the orders around here now."

Nell was on the verge of explosion when, as she leaned over to tap ashes from her cigarette, she saw the sherry glass in my hand. "Do make yourself quite at home."

"She is at home," Ken told her. "The mill belongs to her now."

II

The cigarette snapped in Nell's fingers. Then she said, with an unconvincing attempt to laugh, "Don't be ridiculous, darling. With the exception of a juicy bequest for Dr. Graves and one for Cathy, Aunt Geraldine left her whole estate—Uncle Gerald's estate—to the Harcourts. She told us so when she drew up her will. She said there had been too much bitterness for too long over the Harcourt money and the unfair way it had been handled, and she wanted us to know that it was going back where it belonged."

Ken's eyes narrowed to slits while he looked at her. "She told you about her will six months ago. Since then she has had second thoughts. Ten days ago, she came to the end of her rope and tore up that will. Rather than remain intestate even for a short time, because there is a lot of money and property involved, real estate and stocks and bonds, she drew up a new will that same day, which I have with me now. Cathy is residuary legatee."

The state policemen were silent. Sonia Wenski made a small, derisive sound and her husband's hand clamped over hers so hard it must have hurt her.

"So that's what you've been up to!" Nell said. "You

are responsible for this, Ken. I hope the girl is properly grateful to you. Nice work if you can get it."

Ken's narrow face was amused; Captain Grieg's was noncommittal. Nell turned to him. Anger had ripped off all her restraints, if she was ever a restrained woman.

"It would be interesting to know what Ken Knight and this girl have been cooking up. I'd like to know how that body got in the millstream when the two of them were here instead of at the funeral."

I must have stared at her like an owl, but Ken made no comment. The captain gestured toward the side door and the Wenskis went reluctantly out of the house. After a moment Nell followed, walking with her lovely long stride. Even her back looked dangerous.

The huge room was quiet except for the soft crash and sputter of sparks as a log broke in the fireplace. Captain Grieg was watching Ken. The sergeant, pretending to read his notes, was taking quick looks at the unrevealing face. The only change I noticed was the slight hardening of the angle of Ken's jaw.

"I don't believe it," I said at last. "There must be some mistake. There has to be."

"What mistake?" Captain Grieg asked.

"About the will. Aunt Geraldine would never have left her estate away from her husband's family. She was awfully just."

There was an odd expression on the captain's rather stolid Norwegian face. "You don't think it would be just for you to inherit?"

"She hardly knew me, and I can't believe she intended me to have all that money. She hated family dissension; she had always regretted that her husband and his brother were at odds. She wrote me that she wanted to patch things up. And she said that money made a good patch."

"Patch up what?"

"Family quarrels, I suppose. She said anything for a quiet life, or something like that, whether the quarrels were reasonable or not. And—look, she couldn't have meant me to have everything! She was going to endow an artist's colony. So you see there's bound to be a mistake of some kind."

The side door opened and the Harcourts came back, followed by the couple and shepherded by the lawyer. The Wenskis, after glancing at the captain for permission, went out to the kitchen. Guthrie Harcourt came to sit beside me on the couch. His hands were shaking and he thrust them into his pockets. Maine stood leaning against the mantel, looking down at me. Nell tossed a cigarette butt into the fire and immediately reached for a fresh cigarette. When Arthur Mattheson had lighted it in response to an impatient gesture, she began to pace swiftly up and down the room, her face dead white. Mattheson pulled up a chair near Ken and was watching him with a curious expression. Ken returned the look steadily. The two men, absorbed in that naked but silent enmity, might have been alone in the room.

Everyone was relieved when Dr. Graves came in, walking heavily. "He's been dead only a short time," he told Captain Grieg. "Not more than an hour, possibly less, though it is hard to tell when he has been lying in that cold water."

Captain Grieg's eyes came back to my face. The man must have died only minutes before my arrival, and I was the only person who had seen him before. Both Ken Knight and Arthur Mattheson took a protective step in my direction and then stopped as the police officer's eyes traveled over them.

There was a hint of amusement in Grieg's face when he turned to the doctor. "Murder?"

Dr. Graves was unhappy. "You must have noticed that lump behind his ear. And after your man had finished taking pictures and had got him out of the water, we saw that his pockets were turned inside out. He had been searched before he went into the millstream. There was no identification on him, no billfold, nothing. But whether he was dead or unconscious, I can't tell you until after the autopsy. Of course, if there is water in his lungs—"

The houseman came in with a tray holding a martini pitcher and frosted glasses, a bottle of Scotch, a soda siphon, and a bowl of ice. Maine, moving with his rather languid grace, took charge of it.

"Had you ever seen the man before, Doctor?" Grieg asked.

The doctor shook his head decisively and then looked up with a puzzled expression. "You know I wouldn't swear to that. He's not an unusual type, of course, but I have an impression that I've seen him somewhere." He took his time filling and lighting his pipe while tension grew in the room. Someone was afraid. A dead-end road, Captain Grieg had said. The man was coming to the mill. Someone knew why—someone here in this room.

Then the doctor said regretfully, "No, I simply can't remember."

Wenski, after turning for a swift but deliberate look at me, went back to the kitchen.

Maine, supervising the tray of drinks, asked, "How about you, little cousin?" and I said I'd like a light

Scotch and water. Of them all he was the only one to accept me as though he were genuinely glad I was there. Compared to the restrained caution in Ken and the more powerful but obscurely troubling impact of Arthur Mattheson, Maine's gentle and undemanding attitude of warm affection and obvious approval filled me with gratitude.

Arthur Mattheson had a Scotch that was not so light. The Harcourts and Ken all had martinis. Dr. Graves got himself a glass of sherry from the dining room, and the police, regretfully, refused. They did not, however, show any intention of leaving.

A trooper came in, spoke in a low tone to Grieg, received quiet orders, and then left. After the impression one is given these days of law-enforcement officers rushing in with guns blazing, it was a reassuring sight. We all watched that muted dialogue.

"I understand," Grieg said aloud, "that none of you was able to identify the man."

Guthrie finished his cocktail in two long swallows. "Will you have difficulty in establishing his identity?"

"I doubt it," the captain said. "When a man is killed, there is a reason. Someone had a motive, and motive is hard to conceal when it's strong enough to drive a person to murder. The man came here for a reason. We'll find that reason."

"You mean he came to keep an appointment at the Old Mill," Guthrie said. "Someone lured him here?"

"Not necessarily. He may have been attempting to blackmail someone. That's never a healthy occupation."

"But," Mattheson said, "why in God's name would anyone put him in the millstream where he was bound to be discovered? Why not get rid of him somewhere else?"

"Perhaps the murderer was interrupted and hadn't time to remove the body."

"Perhaps," Nell said smoothly, "it just came natural because he had done it that way before."

There was a moment's pause and then Maine said explosively, "Nell! For God's sake!"

Guthrie stared at his daughter, his mouth opening and closing like that of a drowning fish. Then he handed his glass back to Maine for a refill. The latter gave him a long look and set the glass down on the tray with a decisive little click. Guthrie started to protest and then fell silent.

Wenski opened the swinging door to the kitchen and hovered there, waiting to be noticed.

"What is it?" Nell asked.

"It's about lunch. Would it be all right—that is, just soup and sandwiches? There isn't time to prepare anything else for so many people."

"All right," Nell agreed. I'd have wagered my last penny she wasn't the kind to be lenient with servants, but she smiled at him. "Have Sonia hurry it up, will you? None of us ate much breakfast."

"I'd like to wash before lunch," I said. "I've been on a bus since noon yesterday."

"There's a powder room at the end of the corridor. Aunt Geraldine had it put in when she built on that studio room and bath for the Wenskis," Nell told me.

Ken had been silent for so long that we were all startled when he spoke as though responding to a challenge in Nell's voice. "I assume Cathy will have her aunt's room. It has its own bath, hasn't it?"

"I've already moved in," Nell said.

"Then I suggest," her brother commented, his tone mild, "that you move out again."

"Any fool can see you have fallen for Cathy," Nell

snapped. "And not a bad bargain if you can pull it off. But I'd better warn you that you are too late; Ken has things nicely sewed up. Anyhow, I am not going to be pushed around by—"

"Here, here," Guthrie interposed hastily, "we must not have hard words on a day like this. There is plenty of room in the mill. And it's all in the family, you know."

"Is it?" Dr. Graves asked abruptly. "Sorry, it doesn't really concern me except that I was very fond of Geraldine and there's a limit to everything. I—" He cleared his throat, appearing to be aghast at his own outburst. "I'll report from the hospital as soon as I have completed the autopsy, Captain." He came to touch my cheek lightly with a finger. "Welcome, my dear. There should have been someone to welcome you to Geraldine's home. I know how much she wanted you here."

He went out with a nod to the others, appearing not to notice the unconcealed anger in at least two pairs of eyes. A moment later I heard a motor race and then a car moved slowly around the circular driveway and away from the house.

5

As the houseman came through the swinging door of the kitchen with a big soup tureen, I went along the passageway to the powder room. On my way back, I stopped to look through an open door from the passage into a big studio room. This was the addition I had noticed on my arrival. There was a wide low couch that converted into a bed, a concert grand piano, a record player, shelves and shelves of recordings. Aunt Geraldine must, I thought, have had great faith in young Wenski to spend so much money to provide him with these living quarters. But it could only have been his talent that she admired; no one could have any personal liking for either of the grubby and insolent young people.

Wenski came in with plates of sandwiches. There was a brief hesitation and then we trooped out to the dining room. Guthrie pulled out the chair at the head of the table with something of a flourish.

"I suppose," he said, half smiling, half solemn, "I'm the head of the family now."

Unexpectedly I caught Maine's eyes, alight with laughter and yet imploring me to be patient with his father. While Wenski brought me a bowl of wonderful lobster chowder and passed delectable sandwiches, I found myself liking Maine very much. I smiled at him, attempting without words to assure him that I recognized the absurdity of his father, who had never been head of anything, and to assure him that I would shield the older man as best I could.

Perhaps it was the presence of Grieg and Mendelssohn that made the luncheon so awkward and uncomfortable. Perhaps it was my growing awareness that I was the skeleton at the feast. In any case, I don't remember that anyone talked at all.

Afterward, over coffee in the living room, served by Wenski from the sideboard, Captain Grieg took charge. "Now then, I think we'll have to get things straight. There seems to be some confusion about Mrs. Harcourt's will."

Maine, who had brought his coffee over to the couch and settled down beside me, looked surprised. "I should think—" He broke off.

"Well?" Grieg prompted him.

"Well, there's that body they've just taken away. I should think that would have precedence over anything else at the moment. I don't see what Aunt Geraldine's will has to do with it."

"Perhaps nothing at all. None the less, I'd like to get this thing clear."

Arthur Mattheson took a legal document in a blue cover from his pocket. "This is the will Mrs. Harcourt had me draw up for her. It is dated April twelfth of this year. With the exception of ten thousand dollars to provide for a Town Hall debut for Leopold Wenski, fifty thousand dollars for Miss Briggs and fifty thousand for Dr. Graves, the whole estate is to be equally divided among Mr. Guthrie Harcourt, his son Maine, and his daughter Mrs. Glenn."

This was the first time I knew that Nell was a married woman, though I should have taken it for granted.

Arthur Mattheson was studying Ken's unrevealing face and finding it, I gathered, a fruitless effort.

"I have represented Mrs. Harcourt's legal interests since she came here ten years ago. She was," he smiled warmly, "my first client and the best break I ever had. I had just passed my bar exams and set up for myself." The smile faded. "If, at any time, she was dissatisfied with the way I handled her estate, she never told me so. She even sent me other clients. I thought we were friends. Frankly, Knight, I don't understand this. I didn't understand that story in your paper about a proposed art colony. Why should any of this be done without consulting me? Anyone who knew Mrs. Harcourt must know she was incapable of doing things that weren't straightforward."

Ken had pulled out of his pocket two typewritten pages. "Ten days ago, Mrs. Harcourt tore up the original of that will in my presence. She was angrier than I have ever seen her. I had dropped in to see her with John Turner, a retired lawyer from Burlington who was a great friend of hers. He told her that because of the size of the estate, she should not be intestate even for a few days, so she insisted that he draw up this document then and there. She was—impetuous, you know, and she was extremely angry."

"But why?" Guthrie demanded.

"She told us she had discovered that someone close to her was attempting to convince her that she suffered from delusions and to persuade her to appoint a trustee to handle her estate. In fact, she said there had been at least one attempt made to have her declared mentally incompetent."

"But why?" Guthrie demanded. "That's—" his mouth opened and closed like a drowning fish. "Don't you see that if she really convinced herself of a thing like that, something was very wrong with her."

"So that's what she meant," I said, "about the shadows, about not imagining things, about taking steps."

"What's that?" Nell asked sharply.

"In her last letter—"

"Do you have it?" Captain Grieg asked. "Could you send for it?"

"I brought it with me."

"How foresighted of you," Nell said mockingly.

"But I didn't know about her will," I protested. "I didn't know anything was wrong. I just didn't want anyone in my rooming house snooping around my things."

"Suppose," Grieg interposed, "you give us the gist of the new will, Knight."

"The amount for Dr. Graves remains unchanged; Guthrie, Maine, and Nell each receive twenty-five thousand. Catherine Briggs is the residuary legatee. Her bank is named executor. The Old Mill and its furnishings are also left to her, with the stipulation that she make the place her home for three consecutive months."

"That," Ken explained, reaching automatically for a cigarette as Maine lighted one and exhaled slowly, "was for two reasons: first, to give her time to feel the charm of the place in the hope that she would want to live there; and, second, to set up a foundation to administer the art colony."

"But there is no reference to an artists' colony or to a foundation," Mattheson pointed out.

"Mrs. Harcourt did not expect to die so soon. This new will was simply a safety measure to avoid intestacy." Ken added, "And she knew she could trust Cathy to carry out her wishes."

"In other words," Nell said sharply, "she never intended this will to stand."

"She would undoubtedly have explained what provisions she wanted made for the colony."

"But she didn't have time to get it in writing, did she?" Nell demanded. "Did she? She talks about spending a lot of money for this MacDowell setup and then she dies, leaving everything to Cathy."

My fists tightened until my nails cut into my palms.

Maine expostulated, "Nell! Nell, for God's sake—"

"Is this will legal?" Guthrie demanded. "What do you think, Mattheson?"

"I don't know what to think," he admitted. "I don't understand why Mrs. Harcourt drew up that will without consulting me. I can't understand—knowing her feeling about what she had always believed to be an unfair distribution of the Harcourt money—why she would cut the Harcourts out of practically everything." Again I was aware of the measuring look he gave Ken. "Who witnessed this extraordinary document?"

"Sarah and Leonard Winters. They were the only people available at the time and Mrs. Harcourt was in a tearing hurry to get the thing done."

"She was the most reasonable woman I ever knew," Mattheson said slowly. "In a tearing hurry to dispose of an estate of roughly five million dollars?"

"Who are the Winters?" Maine asked in surprise. "Friends of yours, Knight?"

"Sonia and Leopold Wenski, Mrs. Harcourt's couple."

Guthrie began to smile. "Using false names?"

"No, those are their legal names. The boy thought Americans preferred musicians with foreign names. He uses Wenski professionally."

"I'd like to see the Wenskis," Mattheson said.

Maine went to get them. The girl was nervous and fidgety. Her husband was self-possessed and, I thought, somewhat amused. Both of them agreed that they had witnessed Mrs. Harcourt's will in her presence and in the presence of each other.

"Did she say anything?" Mattheson asked.

"The usual," Wenski said in that unexpectedly deep and assured voice, "about 'my last will and testament.'"

"Nothing else?"

"No."

"Yes," his wife said.

"Shut up, Sonia."

"Someone has to look out for your interests, Leopold. She said that because we were witnesses, we could not benefit by this will, but as soon as the foundation was set up we would be taken care of. Well taken care of. And meantime, she said, we could stay on here so Leopold could practice as much as he likes, and his Town Hall debut was to be paid for."

There was a queer, sly little smile on Sonia Wenski's mouth, which was oddly disconcerting because it was out of character, as though a rabbit had suddenly acquired the characteristics of a fox. "It will be all right, I'm sure." Her rather shallow eyes moved slowly around the room. "No one would want to make trouble for Leopold."

The dishes had been cleared away. In the studio room Leopold began to practice, working on the Schumann "Fantasia in C," playing it at a slow, controlled tempo, every note of the left hand distinct.

"Do we," Nell asked, her voice high, "have to put up with that?"

"You don't have to stay here," Ken reminded her. "Anyhow, you've always hated the place."

"It's our home. Do you mean that Cathy is going to try to put us out?" No one could say that finesse was Nell's strong point.

Mattheson pushed back his chair. "The will must be filed for probate. Are you coming, Knight?" He had no intention of leaving Ken behind him.

Ken looked at me. "You'll want to get unpacked and settled, Cathy." He was making clear there must be no doubt about my staying at the Old Mill. "I'll pick up your suitcase at the bus station and call for you at seven so we can dine somewhere."

He didn't ask me to dine with him. He took it for granted. Arthur Mattheson gave him a quick look, Maine seemed on the verge of protesting and then, after all, he let the lawyer and Ken go without comment.

I never liked anything less than I did being left alone with the three Harcourts. For a moment I thought rebelliously that Aunt Geraldine shouldn't have done this to me. I wanted to assure them that I had no intention of taking a fortune to which I had no moral claim.

Before I could speak, Nell said, "I suppose Ken will raise unshirted hell if you don't get Aunt Geraldine's room. I'll move out for the time being, but get this straight, Cathy. I'm going to fight that will. Ken Knight used undue influence."

"What did he have to gain?"

Nell laughed. "You ask that? What were you and Ken doing here while a man was being killed?"

"But Ken didn't even get there until after I found the body."

Nell gave me a long look. "Among other things, while you were establishing this beautiful rapport, did Ken tell you that he's a widower?"

"Cut it out, Nell," Maine said sharply.

She shook off the restraining hand he had lain on her arm. "Cathy is really the *femme fatale,* isn't she? Every man here seems to be rocked by her, you and Ken and Arthur. Probably Dad, too. But you might set the record straight, Cathy, before you go off the deep end about Ken, even if he's dangling a fortune before your eyes. He doesn't like talking about his wife because she was killed, you know. She was found drowned right out there in the millstream."

Seeing my expression, she laughed. "Let's go up and get you settled in Aunt Geraldine's room."

I gathered up my coat, gloves, and handbag. The latter looked oddly limp. The letters from Aunt Geraldine and the newspaper clippings were gone.

The second floor had an enchantment of its own. Around the open well of the staircase there were grouped chairs and tables, and in one corner a fireplace. Nell threw open the door on the west side. I think I would have known it was Aunt Geraldine's room. It was sunlit and gay; it was comfortable and a delight to the eye, and it was elegant without being stiff.

At the moment, however, it was in a state of split

personality. The delicate, spicy perfume Aunt Geraldine had always used was a part of the texture of the room, but it was overpowered by the heavier perfume that belonged to Nell. The big closet held clothes that obviously were Aunt Geraldine's, though some of Nell's had been crowded in. Nell started to close the closet, then opened it again slowly.

"I just moved in yesterday, so there wasn't time to get rid of this stuff." Her eyes were challenging. "Her things would be too big for you, but I wear the same size."

I made a weary gesture. "I don't want her clothes."

She brightened. "There are some furs, sables and ermine that are still in storage. Well, we can let them wait until we have the matter of the wills straightened out. And Aunt Geraldine's jewelry. She didn't say anything about her jewelry. Gorgeous stuff. You won't try to grab everything, will you?"

I made no comment. I hung my coat in the closet and set my limp handbag down on the dressing table, wondering who had removed the letters and clippings.

"What brought you here?" Nell asked.

"A telegram from Ken Knight."

She started toward the door, turned back to give me a long look. "It's funny the state police were so interested in Aunt Geraldine's second will they seem to have forgotten to ask you about that man in the millstream. You and Ken and the unknown man. Quite a little meeting that must have been."

When she had gone, I sat down on the side of the bed, so limp that it was minutes before I stirred, slipped off my shoes, and got up to remove my black dress, hanging it carefully in the closet. Then I lay down on the bed and pulled a puffy eiderdown quilt over me. I didn't want to go downstairs and face the

Harcourts. Though my conscience was clear enough, I couldn't avoid a feeling of guilt, as though I had deliberately dispossessed them. Nell made no secret of her bitterness and hostility, and I found myself wondering how much of it had to do with the fact that Ken and Maine and Arthur Mattheson had seemed to like me. I had a hunch that, however unscrupulous Nell might be about money, her real stumbling block was men. She was the original girl who couldn't say no.

The afternoon sun was brilliant and reflected in one of the big three-way mirrors, so I closed my eyes. I kept seeing Sonia Wenski's furtive expression as she looked at us, I heard her voice with its implied threat if her husband was not treated well. She knew something about the will and she was uttering a clear warning. Something was terribly wrong. Captain Grieg had known it. Arthur Mattheson had suspected it. Maine Harcourt was afraid of it.

I saw Maine's half-laughing apology over his father's attempt to be established as head of the family. I saw Arthur Mattheson's expression when he first caught sight of me. Beyond all odds, he was the most stunningly attractive man I had ever seen.

One thing I was sure of. I hadn't imagined the shadows. Aunt Geraldine hadn't imagined them. If the place seemed filled with shadows, then they existed and I was going to fight them. I wasn't going to be driven out.

And finally I thought of the man in the millstream, the man who had tried to kill me and who had been struck on the head. The only possible explanation I could see was that someone in this house had hired him to kill me and then had got rid of him because of his dangerous knowledge.

I went over them in my mind: Guthrie with his stubborn effort to make clear that it was all in the family, that there was room at the mill for all of us. Guthrie had dug in his heels and he meant to stay.

Maine? Somehow I rejected the idea without even considering it. Maine was essentially a kind and gentle person, and deeply worried about his father. Was the older man's high color a result of heavy drinking? Maine had certainly refused to give him a second cocktail before lunch.

Nell? I was willing to wager that she was the toughest of the family by long odds. She made no bones of the fact that she intended to fight the will.

Who else? There was Arthur Mattheson and Dr. Graves. Again I eliminated Dr. Graves without hesitation. And the lawyer had not known of Aunt Geraldine's will, so he had no reason for trying to kill me.

Then I was brought up short. Every single one of them, with the exception of Kendrick Knight, had an alibi for the time when the man's body had gone into the millstream. They had all been at the funeral.

My thoughts went round and round. Now and then, I heard someone on the stairs, whose metal treads made any footstep clearly audible. Now and then, I heard muffled voices. And over everything there was the constant beat of the piano. Little as I liked the Wenskis, it was borne in on me that the young man merited whatever help Aunt Geraldine had intended him to have. He was not only a good musician, he was potentially one of the great ones.

He had left the Schumann "Fantasia" now and he was playing Bach. After Glenn Gould, I'd thought no other musician would satisfy me with Bach, but this man's sure touch had complete authority. And then he was playing the Beethoven Sonata, Opus 110, giving it a reading of his own without distortion of the composer's intentions.

Sometime during the afternoon I fell asleep and was awakened by a gentle tap at the door.

"Come in," I said sleepily. But it was not Nell, as I had expected; it was Maine.

"Knight just delivered your suitcase. He thought you might want it. I hope I didn't waken you."

" 's all right," I murmured, and fell asleep again.

6

To my relief there was no one in the big living room when Ken came to take me to dinner. Seeing him in a well-cut suit, a white shirt, and handsome necktie, I was surprised all over again at a man like this settling down to be a country newspaper editor.

I had brought only two dresses with me—a plain black crepe, which I had intended to wear to the funeral, and a soft gray silk, which I was wearing now. Ken's narrow eyes surveyed me with approval and then he held my coat.

"Let's get going, shall we?" he said, and I realized that he was as eager as I was to escape the Harcourts.

The inn had charm as well as good food. When we first went in, I saw Ken take one comprehensive look around and then he relaxed. "No one here who will know us."

"Does that matter?" I asked in surprise.

"People thought a lot of your aunt. I wouldn't like them to feel that you're out on the town on the night of her funeral, and anyone would know who you are because of the resemblance. Sorry, I should have thought of that before."

"Perhaps," I said stiffly, "it would be best for us to leave right away."

"No, that was just a sample of my appalling lack of tact. I want you to stay. And if anyone gets ideas, you'll be your own best advocate." He smiled at me. "Please don't look so upset. I've made every kind of mistake so far, but from now on I'll make it up to you."

When he had ordered a martini and I had a Manhattan, I saw his fingers beat nervously on the table.

"Look," I suggested, "why don't you get a pipe? Wouldn't that be easier than just climbing the wall?"

He laughed. "How right you are! I'll do that tomorrow. Now then, what do you want to eat?"

When he had guided me through the menu, warning me against the lobster but approving of the deviled crabs, I said, "What did you mean when you said you'd got me into this spot?"

Something flickered in his eyes and then he said easily, "You favor the direct approach, don't you?"

"Considering that you believe Aunt Geraldine was murdered, that a man was murdered and put in the millstream, and that he probably tried twice to kill me, I don't think there's much time to waste on the indirect approach."

"Put that way—"

"How would you put it?"

"I hope," he said without amusement, "you aren't given to frequent attacks of directness. Until we know more than we do now about the setup at the mill, it might not be a healthy occupation."

"One thing I'd like to understand is what caused the original trouble among the Harcourts. It disturbed Aunt Geraldine and she planned to set things right. That's why this second will is so unbelievable."

The trouble, Ken explained, when he had ordered a second cocktail for himself, went back a long way, to Gerald Harcourt's father. He had inherited money and snowballed it into a fortune. He had only two children, Gerald and Guthrie. According to Ken, Guthrie was a born con man, the kind of person who was innately dishonest when there was no occasion to be so, even when it was easier and more profitable not to be so. The father had set up a trust fund for him of one hundred thousand dollars, and he was to be paid an income semiannually, as long as he stayed out of the country.

When the father died, Gerald came into his money and he in turn built a powerful business empire. He had educated Guthrie's son Maine at a good prep school and Princeton, and offered to help him get established, but Maine didn't want to go into business. He wanted to write and he had worked for a while in Hollywood and at one of the television studios. Now and then one of the smaller magazines published one of his short stories. Some talent but no drive, Ken summed him up rather disparagingly.

As for Nell, the last thing she wanted was an education. She had run away from school at seventeen with the bouncer from a nightclub.

"Was that Glenn?" I asked.

"Glenn? Oh, no. Glenn was her second husband."

"Second?"

"Twice divorced. The bouncer was just one of— Hell, you can see what she's like. I don't suppose she can help it, but poor Maine spends most of his time getting her out of scrapes."

Ken went on as though he wanted to drop the subject of Nell as quickly as possible. Whether at some point he had fallen for her blandishments, I didn't know. Nell wouldn't be easy to refuse. But at the present time he was keeping her at arm's length, as I had noticed that afternoon, though it was hardly the kind of thing he'd be telling me.

"Well, after Mrs. Harcourt's husband died, she began to get appeals for assistance from his family, especially from Guthrie and Nell. Actually"—Ken was trying to be fair—"I don't know that Maine ever asked for anything. At any rate, she came to the conclusion that she should restore family money to the family. Not very sensible, but very like her."

"I know. She wrote me that she hated family dissension, and she wanted to patch up the quarrels, whether they were just or not. Oh, and that reminds me. I brought with me a packet of her letters, and someone has taken them out of my handbag."

"You're sure of that? You didn't forget them or put them in your suitcase?"

"I'm sure, because when I tore your article about the artists' colony out of the paper while I was on the bus, I could hardly stuff it into my bag because of the letters."

"I don't like that, Cathy. I don't like that at all."

As the waitress glanced in surprise at his grim face, he managed a smile and we devoted ourselves to the deviled crabs, which were all that he had promised.

It was not until we had ordered dessert that Ken said, "Well, that was the beginning of the end. When she had told them what her intentions were, the young Harcourts settled down at the Old Mill, driving out the friends she had so enjoyed. There are only four bedrooms, except in the studio, and they just took over. Guthrie had come back from Europe, which means he must have felt sure no effort would be made to enforce his father's orders that he was to get his income only if he stayed out of the country.

"Little by little, your aunt began to change. Recently it was quite noticeable. She began to complain about shadows in the living room."

66

"I know. She wrote me about them."

Ken's eyes narrowed. "Yes, well, you can see that she was just handing them the ammunition they needed. They said, of course, there were no shadows, that she was imagining things."

"That isn't true. What drove me out of the house this morning after I first got there was shadows moving just at the edge of my vision. And I'm perfectly sound of mind."

"Are you sure?"

As I sputtered, he said hastily, "Sure about the shadows, I mean."

"I am quite sure." I spaced the words distinctly.

"Well, that clears up one point. Anyhow, what happened ten days ago was that Mrs. Harcourt picked up the telephone—there are three extensions, as you may have noticed, but only one outside line. Anyone picking up the telephone can overhear a conversation. What she heard was a man saying that a person could not be declared mentally incompetent without being examined by a psychiatrist and, in the case of anyone as wealthy as Mrs. Harcourt, without an exploration in depth of the whole situation because there was so much at stake."

"Who did a filthy trick like that?"

Ken shrugged. "Your aunt put down the telephone and went through the house like a whirlwind, looking for the other two extensions, but neither of them was in use. She was furious."

I nodded. "So she decided to take steps."

"And that," Ken said, "is when I got you embroiled in this horrible mess. I went along with her when she had Turner draw up the new will with you as residuary legatee. Then we began to talk about it. Five million is a hell of a lot of money to turn over to an inexperienced girl. You'd be easy meat for some fortune hunter."

"Would I indeed?"

"Sorry. I keep making you mad, don't I? Well, anyhow, we discussed the idea of the art colony. I thought if we made a big play of the story, stressing the fact that it was to go into effect at once, whoever was doing this would lay off, because a big slice of the money would be lost to the foundation. But that is where I missed the boat. Someone decided to take action immediately to prevent the money slipping through his or her fingers and hired that man you found in the millstream to get rid of you. I assume your death was to have been announced when it was too late for Mrs. Harcourt to make another will."

"But your article talked only about the foundation. It didn't mention me." Somehow the gingerbread and whipped cream, a spécialité de la maison, as light as a feather, turned to cement in my mouth. I pushed aside my plate.

Whatever else he might or might not be, Ken was swift to grasp the point. For a moment he studied me warily. "Shall I guess?" he asked at length. When I made no reply, he said, "Someone has been doing a nice brain-washing job on you, Cathy. What were you told? That I wanted you to be the heiress in the hope of marrying you? That I—murdered my wife?"

I looked up quickly, looked down again.

The waitress had come back. "Brandy?" she asked. "A liqueur?"

When Ken raised his brows, I shook my head. He ordered Hennessey for himself, and after it came he sat, shaking the glass gently, staring into it as though it held the answer to some problem.

"I did not kill my wife," he said at last as emotion-lessly as though he were reading a timetable. "Grace had an unusual heart condition. Dr. Graves had been treating her for some time." Again seeing my expression, he seemed to read my mind. "True, I haven't much faith in Graves, but Grace liked him. She had confidence in him. She," the glass turned round and round on the tablecloth, "didn't have confidence in many people. She had had polio as a child and though she had only the slightest limp, she was terribly conscious of it and inordinately sensitive. Children can be so horribly cruel, and they had shaken her faith in people and in herself." He lifted the glass and drained it in a few hasty swallows.

"Grace found it hard to believe that anyone could be—genuinely fond of her. She was like a kitten, soft and lovely and wary of strangers. It took several years to make her accept her warm spot in the sun and dare to feel secure and happy. At least, I thought she was happy. We came up here because the crowd I ran with in New York frightened her. She thought they were all brilliant and wonderful and she never dared open her mouth with them. And then—"

His expression changed as though a curtain had been drawn over his narrow, brilliant eyes. "Well, she had a heart attack and fell into the millstream. There was no question at the time of anything else. There was no," his voice trailed away, "reason."

The only thing I was sure of was that this carefully edited story was all that Ken Knight intended to tell me.

"You've got to make up your mind, Cathy. You can't have it both ways."

"What do you mean?"

"If I persuaded Mrs. Harcourt to leave her money to

you so I could marry you and get my hands on it, I wouldn't have hired a killer to eliminate you."

"But who, except you, knew Aunt Geraldine made me her heir in her second will?"

"I hate to keep warning you about the direct approach," he said.

I pushed back my chair and he got up quickly, summoned the waitress, and paid his check.

As we walked through the dining room, I heard a man say, "Did you see that girl? She looks just like Mrs. Harcourt. Must be some relation who came for the funeral."

"Notice who she was with?" a woman replied. "Kendrick Knight, that's who. I'll bet there will be plenty of trouble if Nell Glenn finds out. She staked Knight out for herself."

"Keep your voice down," the man rumbled in the half grunt that passes for a whisper with most men.

"Oh, you're always so cautious! Sometimes I wish you'd come out and say just what you think about something."

"Oh, no, you wouldn't," the man snarled.

We didn't speak again until Ken had helped me into the car and gone around to slide under the wheel.

We were halfway back to the mill when he said abruptly, "Cathy, tell me the truth. Are you afraid of me?"

"I'm afraid," I admitted, "but I don't know what of. Who of."

"Why?"

"What I can't understand," I blurted out, "is how anyone at the mill, or even closely associated with it, could have killed that man today. They all have alibis. They were at Aunt Geraldine's funeral."

"Except me."

70

"Except you." I added, "Why does Mr. Mattheson seem to dislike you?"

"Like Hamlet, I know not 'seems.' He hates my guts. And I hate his. And I should not tell you that if I had any sense at all."

"Why?"

"Probably it will make you fly to his defense. Cathy, let it go for now, will you? This has been a rough day."

"Oh! I just realized why you thought you had been deliberately involved in that man's killing. You think someone put him in the millstream because your wife was found there. Someone wanted to throw suspicion on you."

"It occurred to me."

There were no lights in the mill as we drove up to the front door.

"Did they give you a key?" Ken asked.

"No."

He muttered indistinguishable words angrily to himself. "There's the side-door key in the jar. We'll go around."

We were talking quietly as though neither of us wanted to awaken the sleeping house. "Wait, I'll get the flashlight from the car. You won't know where the switches are and they didn't even leave any lights on for you."

He pressed the flashlight into my hand and we went quietly around the big building to the side door. Ken fished out the key, turned it noiselessly in the lock.

"Will you be all right?"

"Yes, of course. Thank you and good night."

"Good night. Cathy, I don't want to be an alarmist, but it might be a smart idea to lock your door."

I stood inside the dining room, listening to Ken's retreating footsteps. Then I groped my way into the

71

big living room. For a moment I stood trying to re-member the general layout and the position of the fur-niture. I was reluctant to use the flashlight, as though it would reveal my presence. I felt sure I was not alone in the room, but whether it was the sound of breathing or the faint brush of cloth on cloth, I did not know. As I advanced slowly, feeling my way, I felt that the pres-ence was backing away noiselessly. We seemed to be playing some ghostly sort of hide-and-seek.

As my eyes gradually adjusted to the darkness, I thought I could make out a deeper shadow among the shadows of chairs and couches. But what the purpose of this silent stalking was, I had no idea, unless it was designed to frighten me, to drive me away.

All I wanted was to turn tail and run screaming out of the mill and after Ken. Then I saw his car lights switch on, heard the motor turn over, and he was gone.

Reasonless panic had me by the throat. Or perhaps not reasonless. The only excuse I can find for myself was my brush with death two days earlier, my finding of that body in the millstream, and the shocks of the day. It had been the shadows that had driven me out of the house earlier and no one had been there. Everyone had attended the funeral. Except Ken. I came back to that every time.

There was an odd whispering sound, and I stood stock-still. It seemed to me that the pounding of my heart could be heard like Poe's telltale heart, shutting out all other sound. Then I realized what it was, the shushing sound of the swinging door into the kitchen.

A voice whispered, "Don't be a fool. She'll make trouble for you."

"She can't."

"Well, she sure as hell can make trouble for me."

There seemed to be a brief scuffle and then the door shushed again. Now there was only one person in the dark with me. I stood holding my breath. After a moment someone passed me almost without a sound, so I realized that whoever was so near me in the dark was walking in stocking feet. Then I smelled the perfume. It was Nell. But what on earth had she been doing? Actually there couldn't be much doubt about that. She had been holding a secret meeting with Leopold, and obviously it had been much against the latter's will. Somewhat to my surprise, instead of disgust I felt a kind of pity for the tormented woman driven to pursuing men who had no interest in her. I could imagine the savage fury of Sonia if she was aware of Nell's activities.

Nell passed so near me that I could have touched her. She went up the stairs to her room, opened her door, and I saw the light inside. She drew a sharp breath and said, "What are you doing here?"

"I won't ask what you've been doing. Nell, you really are asking for trouble."

"Oh, stop being a bore, Maine. You should have been a preacher. Now get out, will you?" Her voice rose. *"What have you got there?"*

"Aunt Geraldine's pearl necklace. I just found it on your dressing table. She was wearing it when she went to the motel, wasn't she?" After a long moment, Maine repeated, "Wasn't she?"

"She left it in the motel. I brought it home for safekeeping."

"Did you?"

Light spilled out into the hollow square around the staircase and Maine went along to his own room. Nell was silhouetted against the door of her room and then she closed it. I flashed on the light and went swiftly upstairs, not troubling to walk silently. For some reason I believed that the danger, whatever it had been, was gone.

When I had undressed, I slid into bed and then was up again to cross the room and turn the key in the lock. It was a strange thing to do in a private house. My house?

Lying in the dark, I tried to fight my fear of the mill. Something was horribly wrong. I didn't believe the shadows had any supernatural origin; they were caused by human beings. Their purpose was to frighten me as it had been to frighten Aunt Geraldine. But she hadn't scared.

An ill-omened house. What had the newscaster said? Something about it being the scene of the savage Maybury killing. That had been before my time, but a book had recently been published dealing with unsolved crimes, and the Maybury killing had been one of them. A girl named Mavis Maybury had disappeared from her Park Avenue apartment in New York and had been found, weeks later, slashed to death with a heavy knife in the deserted mill. No evidence in regard to her killer had ever been found. She could not be traced from her apartment to the abandoned building, which had long been unoccupied. A handbag containing some forty dollars was found beside her body; she wore several valuable pieces of jewelry. She had not been raped. There was no indication that she had ever taken drugs.

About all that the police had learned was that she had apparently stayed for some days in the mill. There was no sign that she had been held prisoner. There was plenty of food in the kitchen, including caviar. It certainly did not appear to be a kidnaping. No note had ever reached her frantic parents. It became one of the unsolved crimes of the day.

Lying in bed, I thought about the girl hiding in this building or being hidden, and of the maniacal brutality with which she had been carved to death.

Feeling foolish, I reached out to turn on the bedside reading lamp. I simply didn't have the courage to fight it out with the darkness.

As the night wore on and a wind rose, the draperies at the window stirred as though moved by human fingers, the furniture creaked as though someone sat in it, the furnace thumped on and brought me bolt upright.

One thing I felt sure of, I could not spend three consecutive months at the Old Mill—or three consecutive days. I couldn't live like this, shaken by terror, however unreasonable it might be, at every sound, at every shadow. At this rate I'd be jumping when anyone spoke to me. And these people hated me. I was the intruder—the outsider.

To sweat it out, as Aunt Geraldine wanted me to do, seemed impossible. It made me feel as though I had been pushed out onto a high wire and had to balance there to save my life, and there was no net below.

7

The bird song filled the room. I opened my eyes to sunshine and peered sleepily at my watch. Nearly eleven-thirty. It had been daylight when I finally fell asleep.

The exquisite trills were not bird song. Leopold was playing Scarlatti with elegance and precision. When I had bathed and dressed, wishing I had brought a sweater because the house felt chilly, I went to look out of the window.

The millstream glistened in sunlight, so clear I could see the rocks on the bottom. Last night's wind had swept off the last of the leaves, and the trees were stark. The lawn from which the autumn leaves had not been raked shone with the sparkle of frost. The flowers in the cutting garden drooped. It was hard to believe that less than twenty-four hours earlier a man had died violently and been thrown into the stream.

When I went downstairs, there was no one in sight. No attempt had been made to empty ashtrays or dust or straighten the living room.

I pushed open the kitchen door and saw Sonia busy setting a tray with a linen cloth, fine silver, and china. For me?

She turned with a start when I said, "Good morning. May I have some breakfast?"

"I'm just fixing a snack for Leopold. He uses such a

lot of energy. Then I'll make you some fresh coffee. You hungry?"

"Very," I assured her, and pulled out a chair at the kitchen table. "Ask your husband to be careful with that china, will you? It's very valuable."

She darted a quick look at me.

"And I'd like bacon and eggs as well as coffee."

"We usually have lunch by one o'clock." She looked at the time.

"But I'm hungry now. I think we had better come to an understanding, Sonia."

The girl was like a tigress. "Mrs. Harcourt said we could stay. She wanted to help Leopold."

"I'm sure she did. But she expected that you would want to do your part as honorably as she did hers, didn't she? I will carry out her plans for your husband but, unless you are willing to do your share, I won't keep you on here."

She stared at me with stormy eyes. I don't often lose my temper and sound off, but when I do, I mean it. The girl who had been willing to earn the salary Aunt Geraldine paid her was going to earn it for me. Or else. She picked up the tray and went through the side door into the big studio room. As it opened, I heard one of the more impossible Chopin études played as though it were a child's exercise.

It must have been five minutes before Sonia returned, and she wasn't pleased to find me where she had left me at the kitchen table. "You still here?"

"It will save you fixing another tray."

"How long do you expect to stay in Vermont?"

"I don't know. My aunt wanted me to remain for at least three months."

Sonia turned bacon with tongs, broke eggs into the pan. "Mrs. Glenn isn't going to like it."

There was no possible reply to that, not with one of Aunt Geraldine's servants. She stirred a kettle, her very back sullen. But when she looked around and refilled my coffee cup, I noticed that she had begun to smile.

"The living room needs straightening and dusting, and those wilted flowers should be thrown out."

There was a brief battle of wills and then she nodded.

When I had finished breakfast, I said, trying to be casual, not to put too much stress on it, "Has anyone ever said anything about noticing odd shadows in the living room?"

Her shoulders, as she stood at the dishwasher, seemed to stiffen. I waited while she put in my breakfast dishes. "Seems to me Mrs. Harcourt said something once." She put down the lid of the machine with a little click.

Guthrie was sitting in one of the nooks in the living room, the one behind the staircase, reading a newspaper. He stood up, beaming as he caught sight of me. "Good morning, Cathy. You're looking very bonnie today."

Actually I had rarely looked worse. There were blue marks under my eyes from lack of sleep, and my skin felt tight over my cheekbones.

"What you need," he said, "is a spot of fresh air. A nice brisk walk."

It sounded like an attractive idea and I went up for my coat and changed to low-heeled shoes. Guthrie led the way out of the house and headed toward the millstream. For a moment I balked and then I realized that I must get over this distaste. It was only a stream of water, after all—beautifully clean water, and not a place of lurking horrors.

The sun was almost hot, but there was a chill in the air when we got into the shade. The air had that lovely smell it gets in the late fall, particularly in a place still unpolluted by the stenches of civilization.

"Did you have a pleasant evening?" Guthrie asked at last.

"Not awfully, Mr. Harcourt. I was tired and still shocked, I guess."

"You must call me Uncle Guthrie," he said. "We're all family, you know."

It won't be your fault if I don't, I thought, but I made no comment.

"What do you think of Knight?" he asked casually.

"I don't know him at all. But it was kind of him, of course, to look after me."

"Kind?" Guthrie's brows rose quizzically. "My dear, do you have a mirror?" At least there was nothing subtle about Guthrie Harcourt. "Kind," he repeated, when I made no comment. "I'm glad to hear you say that. From what I know of the man, I expected he would regale you with all the Harcourt scandals as soon as he had the opportunity."

It was curious to look at his smiling face and see the eyes so unsmiling and alert behind their horn-rimmed glasses.

"The Harcourt scandals? I didn't know there were any."

Guthrie retrieved his position easily. "There aren't, of course, but as a rule a newspaperman—uh—blows things up. Makes them more interesting. I had an odd impression yesterday that he was trying to drive us Harcourts away from our home." He sighed. "Can't expect a young fellow like that to know what it means for a rootless man like myself to come home at last. At long last. My weary years of wandering are over and

I'm happy to be the old man in the chimney corner." He laughed gently at himself. He had spoken as though he were ninety instead of sixty.

"Come home," he repeated, as though he had been born at the Old Mill. And Aunt Geraldine hadn't even bought it until after her husband's death.

"Knight is an excellent editor. Too bad he confines himself to a village. With a little effort he could probably establish himself in a larger city. Give him more scope."

Scuffing through the leaves, being careful not to slip on the wet ones, which are as dangerous as ice, I made no comment.

"Actually," Guthrie went on, "Knight could probably invest in a bigger paper. I understand his wife left him a packet. Kind-hearted chap. He married this poor little cripple, well, a cripple if not poor. But of course it wasn't for long. A couple of years." He let the thought drop. I was beginning to see that Guthrie was an excellent thought-dropper.

"It's an extraordinary coincidence now that the two of you should have met just when that poor fellow was being killed."

Although we were out in the sun, I shivered. "Cold?" Guthrie asked.

"No. Yes, I think I am. Perhaps we had better go back. I wasn't really equipped for Vermont weather when I came here."

"I expect you'll be glad to get back home," he said, "to your own life and your friends." As I turned toward the house, his hand closed over my arm, his spongy fingers that were soft but unexpectedly strong, tightening. "There's one especially beautiful spot that I want to be the one to show you. People are always delighted with it."

We were moving down closer to the millstream now. Near the house the channel through which it ran was not more than four feet deep. Here it dropped unexpectedly. The ground sloped steeply toward the edge of the bank and the autumn leaves made walking precarious.

Once I almost lost my footing and Guthrie's hand closed more tightly on my arm. "Careful. Watch your step." But he didn't steer me away. We were moving slowly toward the bank, and I was closest to it.

There was a shout and I turned sharply, slipping on wet leaves. Maine was racing along the bank of the stream toward us. "Cathy!" he shouted again.

I had not expected to see the languid Maine move at such a pace. Neither, apparently, had his father. There was a look almost of shock in the older man's face when his son reached us. "I suppose at least the house is on fire," Guthrie said rather acidly. "Or couldn't you wait to see your beautiful cousin again?"

Maine had steadied his breathing and his voice had its usual lazy drawl in marked contrast to that hoarse shout. "Sorry," he said, "but the police have just called. They'd like to see Cathy."

"We were on the point of turning back," his father said as we started toward the house.

Maine gave him a quick look, and I noticed how gray his face was in the bright light.

"They aren't here. They want to talk to her alone at the barracks."

"Oh!" After a moment Guthrie repeated "Oh" rather thoughtfully. "I suppose, my dear, your best bet would be to call Arthur Mattheson and have him look after your interests."

"Later, perhaps," I said.

II

The car into which Maine helped me was a big lux-
urious Cadillac. He saw my expression and his lips
quirked in amusement. "Not my car. This belonged to
Aunt Geraldine. Actually," and he sounded surprised,
"I suppose it is yours now."

I ignored that. So far as the disputed will was concerned, I didn't want to have anything to say. "I wondered, when you came back from the funeral yesterday, how you all managed to get packed into one car.
Now I can understand."

"Oh, we didn't go together. I used my own car, a
little MG; Nell and Dad took this one; the doctor had
his own, of course, and so did Mattheson."

"I had assumed you were all together."

"No, we just happened to converge on the house at
the same time."

"But you were together during the services and at
the cemetery?"

Maine wasn't smiling now. "My dear little cousin,"
he said gently, "don't try to play detective. Leave that
to the trained people." At least he did not pretend not
to know what I was getting at.

"But you were together part of the time?" I per-
sisted.

Maine's hands lay loosely on the wheel; he kept his
eyes on the road. There was just one convulsive moment when his foot pressed hard on the gas pedal, then
he said evenly, "I don't know about the others. This is
an embarrassing thing to have to confess. I have a
nervous stomach and any emotional tension is apt to
upset it. I had to leave the church just as the service
was starting and head for the nearest garage. After that

82

I rode around because it seemed safer to keep out in the fresh air so I wouldn't disgrace myself again."

Between stacks of hay in the fields there were brilliantly colored pumpkins. A roadside stand held pumpkins and apples and bottles of apple cider. Already the season had changed. At any moment now we would awaken to snow and sleet and the savage onset of winter. I shivered, and Maine, who had not appeared to notice me, turned on the car heater.

"Warm in a few minutes," he assured me.

"I didn't bring the right clothes."

"Well, you'll probably be leaving in a few days, so it won't matter too much."

"I don't think I can leave."

"Of course you can. No one could stop you."

"The police could stop me. After all, I'm the one who found that man when everyone else had an alibi. They are bound to wonder."

"Kendrick Knight was there, too. Of all people, I'd have expected him to attend the services for your aunt. He—seemed to be devoted to her. If he didn't go to the mill to meet that man, then why did he go?"

"To see whether he could find any evidence that Aunt Geraldine had been murdered," I said baldly.

For a moment the car was out of control. Then Maine pulled it off the road, leaving the motor running so that I would be warm. He turned to face me, his mouth a white line. "Did he tell you that?"

I nodded.

"In so many words?"

I nodded again.

There was a curious pause while he lighted a cigarette, almost as though he were deliberately taking his time. Then he asked, "Did you believe him?"

83

"What did happen to her, Maine? Why was she in the Old Mill alone when she died?"

"The furnace broke down. We all moved out to a motel while it was being repaired, because, without plenty of heat, the mill is like an Eskimo igloo." He drew deeply on the cigarette and then let out the smoke in a sudden fierce little spurt.

Geraldine, the Harcourts, and the Wenskis all had rooms at the motel. No one kept any track of anyone else. No reason why they should. Probably the Wenskis could alibi each other, if it was necessary, though Sonia would obviously stick her hand in the flames for her husband. The others had separate rooms.

"My father snores," Maine commented briefly.

No one knew how Ken had just happened to go to the mill, where he found her, although he had been told that they had left the place. No one knew why Aunt Geraldine had gone back. The motel was four miles away. Her car had been left in front of her room, not at the mill, though she had never been an enthusiastic walker. She had also left behind a pearl necklace. Or had she? I thought I was beginning to understand something of Maine's torment. He trusted neither his father nor his sister.

He lifted one hand, dropped it on the wheel again, reached for another cigarette. "Well, there it is." He put the car in gear again and drove me to the barracks without another word.

III

It's a pity that only bad news is supposed to be news: police brutality, and the swinging of nightsticks, and careless shooting, and manhandling. It all happens, of course. I've seen it myself on television. But I'd like to have the other side get a fair deal: the police who help bring babies into the world, who uphold law and order without unnecessary violence, who are soft-spoken and courteous, who endure to the breaking point the insults and jibes and incitement to violence of neurotics, young punks, and extremists.

Captain Grieg and a sergeant whom I had not seen before got to their feet when I entered the barracks. Grieg looked as though he hadn't had much more sleep than I had. As it turned out, he hadn't had any.

"You look a bit chilly, Miss Briggs. Not used to our Vermont weather." He glanced at the sergeant. "How about some coffee for Miss Briggs?" He nodded to Maine. "Thanks for bringing her here. Will you wait in your car or shall we see that she gets home?"

Maine took his dismissal gracefully. "I'll wait in the car."

"Seems to be a pleasant guy," Grieg commented when Maine had gone out.

"Very pleasant," I assured him.

The rather shy young sergeant brought me a cup of steaming coffee and a thick bowl of sugar and pitcher of cream. Grieg leaned back in his chair.

"Well, Miss Briggs, we've been spending a lot of time on you," he said genially.

I had lifted the coffee cup. Now I set it down in surprise. "On me?"

He grinned. "People who go about finding bodies—" As my jaw dropped, he chuckled. "Okay, Miss Briggs. Nothing to worry about. First, we traced your bus trip. Quite a lot of trouble you ran into. We know when you left home and when you got to Milltown, so you seem to be out."

85

"Seem?" This time I was really indignant.

"Now there's another thing. Ever hear of a man named Tim Cooper?"

I shook my head.

"Positive of that?"

I nodded.

"Tim Cooper is the man you found in the millstream and, incidentally, Doc Graves says he was dead when he went in. We have his fingerprints and quite a nice little record."

The genial look clouded. "Sometimes I wish sentimental people would see some of these records! Oh, well—" He abandoned hope of common sense with a helpless gesture. "Tim Cooper has been in trouble off and on, mostly on, for about eighteen years. Juvenile delinquent. Stole cars. Assault and battery. Mugging. Twice involved with murder, but each time he got off with a technicality. I don't suppose he's done an honest day's work in his life, and he hasn't served any time at all. If someone had done more than slap his wrist when he went off the beam the first time, he might have been a decent guy.

"What took most of the night was checking out Cooper's visit to your home town. Night checking. They take in the sidewalks out there, don't they, and everyone seems to be in bed by ten o'clock. But we got someone who saw him on the flight, someone at the Curtis House where he had breakfast who identified the mug shots. He was the man who dropped that sign that nearly obliterated you. We haven't found anyone who noticed him in the cafeteria. We got hold of the man Mitchell who says you came to see him about a job." Grieg grinned. "You made quite an impression." The smile faded. "We have a confirmation of the death of the woman by cyanide in the cafeteria.

But we haven't traced Cooper back here. We still don't know which one he came to see. You're positive he mentioned no names?"

"Only Aunt Geraldine's. If you've found out all that, no wonder you had no sleep!"

He looked surprised. "Usually the public assumes that the police doesn't need sleep. Or that it is always asleep. All sympathy is welcome."

"But why did the man come to the library?"

"That part is easy enough. He had to know what you looked like."

"Oh!" I caught my breath.

"You see, it was practically set up for him. We don't know what he had in mind when he went out there, but he saw your ad, noticed that the Mitchell outfit was new in town so you wouldn't be likely to know them, arranged to get you under that scaffolding at the right time. And, apparently, he had the cyanide as a second line of attack if the first one failed."

I shivered. "There's only one possible motive, isn't there? That second will of Aunt Geraldine's. But no one knew about it except—"

He said casually, "I understand you had dinner with Kendrick Knight last evening. You know, I don't want to give you any gloomy ideas about Milltown, but I suggest that, until we get this thing wrapped up, you don't go out unless you are with at least two people."

"Are you suggesting that Kendrick Knight is not to be trusted?"

Grieg took his time. "No. Not really. Personally I think he's a nice guy. I like his paper. I like his quality. But, well, damn it all, we've got to face facts, Miss Briggs. He seems to have engineered that second will for your benefit. There's no getting around the fact that Mrs. Harcourt died before anything could be done

about that art colony. And—I don't like coinci-
dences."

"You mean his wife's drowning?"

"You've heard of that? Happened two years ago.
Sweet little woman." Grieg pushed away his coffee
cup. "Wealthy. Left everything to her husband except
a nice bequest for Dr. Graves. Very nice bequest.
Fifty thousand dollars."

"Dr. Graves's patients seem to have a high regard
for him," I said. "At least the women patients do."

Grieg looked at me quickly and shook his head. "It
won't do, Miss Briggs. We can't drag Graves into this.
He is the medical examiner and highly regarded in his
profession. His patients swear by him. He has no family and he makes more money than he spends. He
owns that big house on Main Street, the Georgian one.
No, it won't do. Anyhow, we have one grim fact to
face. The only one of the whole shebang who has no
alibi for the murder of Cooper is Knight. The rest were
all together at the funeral."

"Are you sure of that?"

He stared at me. "Now what—"

"I had assumed, as you did, that they were together,
first at the church and then at the cemetery. Then I
remembered Mrs. Glenn asking the Wenskis when
they came back what had taken them so long. And yet
they arrived at the mill only a few minutes after the
others and, according to them, they had had to walk
back. And Maine told me while we were driving here
just now that they weren't together; he drove his own
car; Mrs. Glenn and her father had Aunt Geraldine's
Cadillac; Dr. Graves and Mr. Mattheson each went
alone. And Maine doesn't know whether they were
together at any time because he has a nervous stomach

and he had to leave the church in a hurry because he was sick. He didn't go back."

Grieg looked at me and then at the sergeant.

"And it's the same for the time when Aunt Geraldine died. Except for the Wenskis, who can alibi each other—or would, in any case—they weren't together; they can't vouch for each other."

"You've been talking to Knight. He's the one who is sold on the idea that your aunt was pushed down those stairs."

"You know perfectly well that I've been talking to him. But it's Maine who made me realize that no one has an alibi."

"You seem to have been learning quite a lot." There was nothing particularly complimentary in Grieg's voice.

"If I've been snooping," I said hotly, "I have plenty of reason. Someone wants me to be dead."

He looked at me and made no comment.

"And whether you believe it or not, I seem to be developing a strong sense of self-preservation, Captain. I want to be alive for a long, long time."

"Let's hope you will be. Any other tidbits you've picked up?"

If he hadn't taken that tone, I probably would have told him everything I knew or suspected. I'd have told him of Nell's threat that she would break the will; of Maine wondering how Nell had got hold of Aunt Geraldine's pearl necklace; of Sonia's rigid silence when I had first mentioned the shadows in the living room; of that obscurely terrifying moment when I had believed that Guthrie Harcourt meant to send me pitching into the millstream if Maine had not come racing toward him, shouting a warning.

89

Instead, like a fool, I clammed up. Grieg paid no attention to my sulks. Patiently he took me over the events since I had reached the mill. At last he stood up, nodded, and yawned widely.

"Okay, I'll call it a day. But—you aren't planning to leave here, are you? Don't go without telling us."

"Not without telling you," I agreed.

"That's a good girl. We'll want you at the inquest on Cooper. Anyhow, I don't like seeing good-looking girls get into trouble, even if they sort of stick their noses in where they don't belong."

8

Maine gave me his quick delightful smile as he came around to open the car door for me. "How was the inquisition?"

Annoyed as I had been by Captain Grieg, I found myself coming to his defense. "They were very courteous and considerate."

"No third degree?"

"All done by kindness. And poor Captain Grieg was practically out on his feet because he had been working the whole night."

"To some purpose, I hope," Maine said lazily.

"To a great deal of purpose. He had checked on my bus trip and he provides me with an alibi for the killing of that man in the millstream."

"Good Lord!" Maine was disgusted. "He couldn't possibly have believed you had anything to do with that."

"Perhaps not, but it's nice to know that he is sure about me. Oh, and he knows who the man was, a criminal named Tim Cooper with a long record, and Captain Grieg found out he was the one who tried to kill me back home."

The car jerked and Maine straightened it again. "Good God! What are you saying?"

"Oh, I guess you weren't there when I was telling the police." I described my curious and terrifying en-

91

counters with Tim Cooper. "And then I came to the mill and found his body. So there's no evading the fact that someone at the mill hired him to get rid of me." My hands were gripped hard together on my lap, but I kept my voice steady. "Is there, Maine?" The speed had dropped from fifty to thirty to fifteen. Maine was staring ahead of him. "Is there?" I repeated.

Minutes passed before he said, "Nothing must happen to you, Cathy. You've got yourself a watchdog."

"How could you possibly protect me?"

He maneuvered slowly through a narrow covered bridge and then pulled up so that we faced a noisy little river rushing over big boulders. Beyond the bridge a dirt road wandered out of sight around a hill toward some isolated farm house. It was so picturesque, so like a postcard view of rural Vermont, that I found it hard to believe I was actually seeing it. All that was missing was a horse-drawn hayrick with a couple of rosy-cheeked children.

Maine turned to face me, one arm stretched along the back of the seat, his finger touching my shoulder lightly. "I wish you would marry me."

"Marry—" I began to laugh. "I met you for the first time yesterday. Are you crazy?"

There was no answering laughter in the handsome face. "Let's take first things first." He looked not at me but at the self-important, bustling little river. "And the first thing is to make sure you stay alive. The best way I know to assure that is for you to marry me."

"Why?"

"Because, once you are married, there will be no advantage to—anyone—in killing you. There would be no one who could profit by your death."

"Except," I pointed out, "you."

92

He met my eyes levelly. "Except me. Well, Cathy?" I shook my head.

"I wouldn't expect—that is, later, of course, you could get a divorce or an annulment or whatever, and I wouldn't fight it. That is, if I couldn't find a way to make you care a bit about me by then. I just want you safe, and there's no other way that I can see."

I shook my head again. "Which one is it, Maine?"

That jolted him. "Good God! I don't know, Cathy. I don't know." After a moment he demanded, "Do you believe that?"

"I don't know," I said wearily. "I just can't be sure about anything. I'd like to believe in you, Maine. Honestly I would."

His mouth twisted wryly. After a long time he said, "If you won't marry me, Cathy—and I believe it would be your wisest course—will you leave here tomorrow and go back home?"

"I can't leave here. The police want me to stay at least until after the inquest on Cooper."

"Then go as soon as they give you permission."

"And ignore that stipulation in Aunt Geraldine's will about staying at the mill for three consecutive months?"

"Yes."

"And lose everything."

"But not your life," Maine said quickly.

"How do you know that? I wasn't safe at home. And there are other killers for hire like Cooper. Anyhow, I'd not only be disregarding Aunt Geraldine's wishes, I'd be surrendering tamely to the person who killed her." Maine's hands jerked once on the wheel and then were still. "The person who killed Cooper and nearly killed me."

"Is the money worth the risk?"

"I'm not going to be bluffed." Again I felt as though I were taking the first step onto a high wire, balancing dizzily over space, and my mouth was dry.

"Then God help you." Maine started the car and inched his way back through the narrow bridge and onto the highway, out of the past and into the present. "Are you in a hurry to go back," his voice was normal again, "or do you mind stopping at the drugstore in town?"

"I'd like to. I need toothpaste and a showercap."

While Maine had a prescription filled, I bought toothpaste and a showercap and stood looking at a display of paper costumes for Halloween. Maine came toward me, and I was aware again that he was a very good-looking man. He paused beside a bin that was filled with packages of candy for Trick or Treat night.

"Every year your aunt made a big thing of Halloween and Trick or Treat night. It started, I think, because she wanted to replace the ugly old horror stories about the mill by a kind of lighthearted magic and gaiety. She set up witches on broomsticks and had jack-o'-lanterns in the window, and every year she gave a little party for children. I've heard her tell about it. She would wear a witch's costume and greet all the children personally. No telling how many of them may come by this year, not knowing of her death. What do you think? Shall we get some candy for any kids who happen to come around?"

"Of course. Do whatever you think she would have liked. And get a costume, too."

Maine collected some things and looked around for a clerk. She was out of sight behind a high counter, waiting on a customer whom I could not see. Then she came around to smile at Maine. "I'll be with you in a minute."

"No hurry." He slipped his hand under my arm. He smiled down at me. "We're fine as we are."

The girl looked from Maine to me. "Why, you must be related to Mrs. Harcourt." Then she noticed Maine's air of unmistakable proprietorship. "Congratulations, I'm sure."

I was too angry to say anything. Maine continued to smile fatuously at me until the clerk brought his package and change. Out in the car I turned on him.

"What on earth made you act like that?"

"Protecting my interests," he said coolly, and he refused to discuss the matter further.

When I said, still raging, "If this is like most small towns, everyone in the place will hear within twenty-four hours that we are engaged."

"That, of course, was the general idea." Maine drew up before a roadside stand and got out to select a couple of big pumpkins. When he had deposited them carefully on the back seat, he declared, "I'm the world's best jack-o'-lantern man. I'll scoop these out and cut some faces—Oh, candles! I must get candles. And maybe we can talk Sonia into making some of her wonderful pumpkin pies."

It was on this cheerful and impersonal note that he drove me back to the mill. I had been adroitly out-maneuvered. Of course I could always deny any engagement, but rumor was harder to fight.

The living room had been straightened and dusted; the wilted flowers were gone; the ashtrays had been emptied and washed. For once the piano was silent. The only sound was a tinkle of glass against glass in the dining room. Guthrie came in. His color had heightened and he had obviously been drinking. Maine made a small sound of distress and then he appeared to ignore his father's condition while he displayed the pumpkins, the candies, and the costume with its mask.

Guthrie, who had given each of us a sharp, hard look, relaxed and beamed at us. "So you weren't held in durance vile. Now I hope the police will let this poor child go back home in peace."

"Not until after the inquest." I started up the stairs, turned back. "Oh, by the way, they have identified the body in the millstream. He was a criminal named Tim Cooper."

There was no change in Guthrie's expression that I could see. In my room I opened the closet to hang my coat. It was empty except for my one extra dress. Aunt Geraldine's clothes had been removed. Nell had wasted no time. I was surprised at the wave of furious anger that burned along my veins, not for the clothes but for this greedy haste to grasp what had been Aunt Geraldine's.

When I went downstairs again, I called Sonia and planned menus with her. Somewhat to my surprise, but greatly to my relief, I found her amenable and even eager to please. Apparently my threat of sending her away had scared her badly. She would never consent to being separated from the husband she adored. We talked about weekly marketing, where the best meats were to be found, and the daily milk delivery, all in the utmost amity.

Nell, strolling down the stairs in brown slacks and a form-fitting yellow sweater, looked at us where we sat in the nook behind the fireplace.

"Quite the gracious lady of the house," she drawled. "By the way, Dad has asked Arthur Mattheson to dinner tonight. I hope you won't have him thrown out because the invitation did not come from you."

"Don't be silly!" I spoke more sharply than I had intended. "Naturally—" I broke off. I had meant to say that naturally the Harcourts were to treat the mill as their own home, but the words stopped in my throat. For all Guthrie's insistence, there wasn't room for all of us. Their presence would mean a constant tug of war, and I didn't think I could bear that. I was no more delighted by the presence of a plague of locusts than Aunt Geraldine had been.

Nell looked down at me sardonically where I sat tongue-tied, unwilling to bring the issue to a head. "Naturally Dad is free to issue invitations? Or naturally Arthur is welcome? Quite bowled you over, didn't he? Take a word of advice. Be satisfied with Maine and Ken. Keep your hands off Arthur." Before I could answer, she turned to Sonia. "Send Leopold up to my room, will you? That tap is leaking again. It drives me mad." She reached out to fill her cigarette case from the box on the table, gave an amused look from Sonia to me, and went back up the stairs.

"She'd better get her hands off Leopold or I'll make her sorry she was ever born," Sonia muttered.

"Now about dinner tonight," I said hastily, and she bent over the notebook in which she was jotting down menus and shopping lists.

When she had finished, she shut the little notebook. "It's like working with Mrs. Harcourt. You knew where you were with her. She was always business-like."

"She was also kind," I said. "Certainly she was kind to your husband."

Sonia nodded and her pasty skin glowed so that she

97

was almost pretty. "Someone brought him to her and had him play and she knew right away how good he was. He'd run out of money and he's an orphan with no one to back him and there would be the expense of a recital and all that, and he couldn't even practice where he was living in a room at a boarding house. That's where we met. I was cook there. Well, Mrs. Harcourt had built on the studio. She'd meant it to be a party room, but she offered it to us, and got the piano, and said we could have two hundred dollars a month for our expenses, though she even provided food. But Leonard—I mean Leopold—thought the money should be earned, and I guess he was right. So I do the cooking and he's houseman."

"And that's how you happened to witness the will."

"We were the only ones around that day, except for Mr. Knight, and Mrs. Harcourt explained that we couldn't be in the will if we were witnesses, but she promised it wouldn't make any difference about her helping Leopold until he was launched on his career."

"If I have a chance to carry out her wishes, it won't make any difference," I promised her.

Sonia nodded. "I guess you mean it, too. That's what Mrs. Harcourt said, that you were the only person she could trust implicitly and you were so much like her that she knew how you would act."

The thing that had gnawed at me like a fox under my cloak was that only Ken had known of the change in the will, so only Ken had any motive for hiring Cooper to get rid of me. Now my heart lifted. Sonia had known, too, and probably her husband as well.

"Sonia, whom did you tell about that second will?"

"No one." She said it too quickly, trying to hold my eyes, her own wide and limpid with honesty.

"Please tell me. Please."

"I never said a word to anyone."

"You don't understand how terribly important this is. Perhaps Mrs. Harcourt didn't die accidentally, Sonia. It's just possible she was killed because of that will. So it matters horribly who knew about the provisions."

There was more than shock in Sonia's face. There was stark horror and the beginning of terror. "No! No!"

"Someone killed that man whose body was found in the millstream. He had tried twice to kill me. I think he must have been hired by someone here—because of the will you witnessed."

Sonia pressed her clenched fist against her ashen lips and then turned to run stumbling out into the kitchen.

II

Fighting an uphill skirmish all the way, Maine seemed to be hell-bent on making the evening cheerful, though the circumstances couldn't have been more unpromising. He was taking on what was his father's accustomed role. Guthrie had continued to drink heavily all day and, though he could still walk and talk without much difficulty, he was unusually silent.

Nell had changed for dinner to an exquisite dark-red dress that brought a muttered protest from Maine, so I knew it must have been part of Aunt Geraldine's wardrobe. She wore more make-up than usual, but it accentuated rather than concealed a haggard appearance. She also wore a beautiful necklace of matched pearls.

For a moment, when Maine saw them, I thought there was going to be a scene. Then he turned away from her abruptly, went out into the kitchen, and returned with the two pumpkins, which he had scooped out, and in which candles flickered, showing the eyes, nose, and jagged teeth. He set them carefully in the windows on either side of the front door.

"Oh, for God's sake!" Nell said irritably. "How childish can you get?"

"Aunt Geraldine had made it part of the tradition of the mill. There may be kids coming who would be disappointed." He went out and returned with a basket filled with candies.

Leopold brought the drink tray into the living room. After a quick check, Nell said shortly, "You forgot the Scotch." The doorbell rang and he set down the tray and started for the door. "Get the Scotch, Leopold. Sonia can admit Mr. Mattheson."

"She's just getting ready to serve dinner."

"But she'd do a lot to keep you here, wouldn't she?" Seeing the flare of anger in his face, Nell laughed. She really liked to draw blood. She raised her voice. "Sonia!"

Sonia pushed open the kitchen door.

"Didn't you hear the bell? Open the door."

"I thought Leopold—"

"He has something else to do. He is carrying out my orders."

Before the smoldering girl could speak, Maine said quickly, placatingly, "Hey, wait a minute. I got you a costume, Sonia. Let's get into the spirit of the thing." He helped her to adjust the paper witch's costume and mask with a huge beaked nose, while she laughed in delight and I realized for the first time how young she was, just a girl, several years younger than I, and probably a girl with no memory of youthful games.

The paper dress rustled in a gust of wind as she

opened the door. Arthur Mattheson came in quickly and helped her to push the door shut.

"Storm coming up," he said as Guthrie took his coat. He looked at the witch's costume and at the lighted pumpkins. "Keeping up the tradition. I'm glad of that. Mrs. Harcourt would have been pleased. Everything is just the same, I see."

"Not everything," Sonia said, and went back to the kitchen. I saw her husband's eyes follow her, and I didn't like their expression. Then he opened the new bottle of Scotch, filled the tantalus, and stepped back so Maine could serve the drinks. The kitchen door swung behind him and I could hear outraged whispers in the kitchen sounding like a giant whistling teakettle.

Arthur had come to smile down at me, his presence like an electric current in the room. "Was this your idea?"

"No, it was Maine's."

"I hope you don't mind my coming."

Not only Nell but both the Harcourt men were watching me.

"Of course not." I turned casually to toss some pine cones onto the fire. For the first time I wished that I was a smoker. The ritual of lighting a cigarette is a nice filler of time.

Nell stretched out her hand and Arthur went to take it. She indicated the chair beside her with a peremptory motion.

"Actually," Guthrie said, speaking clearly enough, with just a touch of thickness in his voice, "I asked you to come because I thought it would be a good idea to have you here professionally as well as socially." He refused a cocktail, waited until Maine had distributed the glasses, and then went to pour himself a Scotch

and soda. Judging by the color, it must have been prac-
tically straight Scotch. He avoided Maine's eyes.
"This poor child must need some sound legal advice.
She has been with the police most of the day."

"Oh, it's not that bad," I protested. "Not more than
an hour and a half."

"But why didn't you send for me?" Arthur asked.
"That's what I'm for, you know. Like that fellow in
the television ads whom you call on in time of trouble
to fix the drains."

I laughed. "But they were really very nice. I didn't
need anyone to defend me against them. Actually, I
felt that they wanted to protect me."

"What from?"

There wasn't, so far as I could see, any reason for
not telling the truth. So I started with Cooper's attempts to kill me, told how the police had identified
him and traced his criminal record. It seemed probable
that he had come here either to blackmail someone or
to ask for further orders. And, I went on steadily, it
was possible that Aunt Geraldine's death had not been
an accident.

Maine had come to sit beside me on the couch. Arthur looked at him, a queer expression on his face.
Then he said, "I wish you had told me all this before.
Of course, now that I know the situation, I'll watch
you so that no one can touch you." There seemed to be
a warning in his voice, and I felt that he probably
thought, as I did, the danger that threatened me might
lie within this room.

Nell got up and perched on the arm of Arthur's
chair, slipping her arm casually around his shoulders
as though to balance herself. He stirred uneasily and
then his glass tipped, spilling Scotch on his trousers,
and he got to his feet.

"Damn! What a clumsy ox. Do you have a towel, Maine?"

"Help yourself. Powder room at the end of the passage," Maine said lazily. He did not leave his place beside me.

Arthur went down the hallway and Nell, picking up her cocktail glass, went to stand in front of the fire. "How much truth is there in that story," she demanded, "and how much is a pretty little fantasy?"

"Of course I know what happened to me back home, and so do the police. As to why Cooper came here and was killed, there's only guesswork. And about Aunt Geraldine—"

"That I don't believe." Nell was white. One hand went up to touch the pearl necklace, as though it were a talisman, and I saw Maine watch the hand, watch the fingers tighten over the gleaming pearls, relax, and fall again. "No one would have wanted to hurt Aunt Geraldine."

Someone laughed. Sonia had opened the kitchen door. She looked at Nell and laughed again. Then Leopold seized her arm, dragged her out to the kitchen, and the door swung shut. There was a sharp crack whose meaning could not be mistaken; he had struck his wife across the face with his open hand.

"You'll be sorry for that," she cried. "How long do you think you can shut me up? You or anyone? Things have changed now."

There was a faint tinkle on the telephone and then, without further warning, the lights went out.

9

Leopold, his impassive face revealing no trace of the quarrel with Sonia, brought candles. There were a great many of them, but in the huge, irregular space of the room they accomplished little more than to enable us to move around without falling over the furniture.

"Dinner is served," he announced when the last candlestick was in place.

Guthrie stood up, staggered, and clutched at the back of his chair for support. He gave a quick crafty look around him. "Not drunk," he said emphatically. "Dizzy spell. Martyr to them all m' life."

Maine, his face set, eased his father into the chair to which he was clinging. "He can't—"

"I know. You'll take his place, won't you?"

He smiled at me. "With very great pleasure," and he moved to pull out my chair at the table before Arthur could do so.

My chair faced the living room, its back to the uncurtained window that opened on the screened porch. Though there could be no one outside, I felt exposed and insecure. There was a cold draft from somewhere, and the thought of that window, of the darkness beyond, of the dim living room with its inadequate lighting, made me shiver. At that moment I would have given anything to be transported back to my uncomfortable little room in the boarding house.

The meal was a gastronomic triumph, which should have helped to raise our spirits. Then, as children began to arrive, and Sonia, in witch's costume and mask, went back and forth to open the door, distribute candies, and laugh at the odd costumes, there was really a spurious kind of gaiety. I tried hard, heaven knows, and so did Maine. When Nell became aware that Arthur was watching Maine and me, a speculative expression on his face, she took over the conversation, determined to force his attention on her.

Once Arthur raised his voice. "What is it, Cathy? What in the world are you staring at?"

"I thought—there seemed to be some odd shadows in the living room. I wish the lights would go on."

Arthur reached out to cover my cold hand with his warm one. "You're tired and you've been under a strain. Anyhow, the living room has too many nooks to be properly lighted. There are always shadows. This is an odd house, you know, with an odd history. I've often wondered, charming as she eventually made it, why Mrs. Harcourt wanted to live here."

"You don't like it?"

"Not to live in," Arthur admitted. "Too many ghosts."

Nell laughed. "Don't tell me you're afraid of ghosts, darling."

"Not afraid, of course. But there are places that seem to attract violence. Look at the history of this one." He broke off to help himself to roast turkey and Sonia's chestnut dressing, which was a triumph. "It was abandoned in the first place because the owner of the mill strangled his wife in a drunken rage. No one wanted to take it on, and in time it got a reputation of being haunted."

Nell protested, "Arthur darling. Don't be absurd."

"Probably," he said, "tramps used it as a shelter, so people saw shadows at the windows, flickering lights, all that; anyhow, they gave it a wide berth. And then, of course, there was the notorious Maybury killing. No one ever knew or ever will know why the girl was brought here, who brought her, and how she happened to be murdered in so savage a way, literally slashed to pieces with a knife."

Maine set down his own knife with a clatter. "Cut out the gruesome details. You're taking away my appetite."

Arthur looked at him, looked down to butter a hot roll. "Squeamish?" he asked gently. "You continue to surprise me, Maine."

There were giggles outside the house, and the bell rang. Sonia came through to answer it, the paper costume rustling as she walked, the mask with its great beaked nose casting a grotesque shadow.

Cold air swirled around our feet as she opened the door and gave a half-startled shriek. From where I sat, I could see the three hoboes at the door. Then I noticed the flaming red noses and realized they were just more children in costume.

As Sonia came back through the dining room, Arthur said, "That chestnut stuffing is perfect. You could make your fortune with it."

She paused for a moment, turning her head so that I could see the glittering eyes behind the mask, looking at Nell, and caught for a moment in the light of a candle. "I intend to make my fortune," she said, and went back to the kitchen.

"Do you really intend to keep that girl on here?" Nell demanded.

"It's what Aunt Geraldine wanted," I said.

"What Ken Knight tells you she wanted," Nell snapped.

"But why would he do that if it isn't true?"

"He's an odd chap," Arthur commented. "I've never understood why he was content to bury himself here. Of course, before his wife's tragic death, he had a reason. He felt, or said he felt, that she needed isolation. But after that, with all her money—"

"I didn't know you had ever met her," Nell said sharply.

"Yes, she was a sweet creature, a helpless little thing. Very pathetic."

"With all that money?"

"It couldn't save her life," Arthur said. "In fact—" He broke off quickly.

Ken had been right, I thought, in saying that Arthur Mattheson hated his guts. Was it because of Ken's dead wife? Had she felt Arthur's immense charm?

"Can't we," Maine protested, "inject a little festivity into this dinner, for God's sake, instead of sitting on the ground and telling sad stories of the deaths of kings?"

"If that," Nell commented, "is a sample of your prose style, I don't wonder you can't get your stuff published."

"The style is Shakespeare's. If you hadn't stopped reading at about the fourth-grade level, you would have recognized it."

"Children," Guthrie expostulated unexpectedly from the living room, startling us all. For a man who had been practically out on his feet, he sounded alert.

Even Sonia's delectable pumpkin pie didn't help the overcharged atmosphere at the table. When we had moved into the living room, Guthrie began to take some interest in his surroundings, and accepted with unexpected meekness the coffee Maine brought him.

As Nell started purposefully toward Arthur, he picked up his cup and came to sit beside me. "Now let's hear about your interview with the police. Oh, first you had better give me a retaining fee. Do you have a dollar?"

"Apparently she has five million of them," Nell reminded him tartly.

I went up to get my handbag, wondering again who had removed the letters and clippings, and went back to give Arthur four quarters, which he solemnly placed in his pocket.

"Now then—"

So I described my interview with the police. Occasionally Arthur asked a question but, for the most part, he just listened.

"And you found the man dead when you got here," he said at length.

"At least the police know I couldn't have killed him. Not possibly."

"How nice for you," Nell murmured.

"But, my dear girl," Arthur said, troubled, "you see, don't you, where that leaves us. Everyone associated with the mill and with Mrs. Harcourt has a cast-iron alibi for the time when this man was murdered. They were all at the funeral services except for Kendrick Knight."

There was a sharp ring at the door and Sonia went to open it.

"Enter a murderer," Maine said lightly.

But it was Ken Knight who came in, peering in astonishment at the darkened room, the witch's costume, the grinning pumpkins and flickering candles. He entered on a violent gust of wind that snuffed out some of the candles and set the flames of others on a slant. His eyes sought me out and he seemed to relax a little.

"Sorry, barging in like this, Cathy; your telephone is out of order and I got to worrying. I thought I'd better check up."

"What did you imagine would happen to her?" Arthur asked dryly.

"I don't know." Ken could hardly ignore that hostile atmosphere. No one asked him to sit down. Both Arthur and Maine remained standing, waiting politely for him to leave. "Well, if you're all right—" He turned awkwardly toward the door.

"You mustn't worry about Cathy," Maine told him. "She is my responsibility, you know."

Guthrie gave his son a startled look and then he beamed. "My dear boy!" He pumped his son's hand.

Nell's hand crept up to touch the pearl necklace. She was smiling. "Well, so that's it! Just one happy family."

"Cathy," something in Ken's voice brought my eyes quickly to his face, "is this true? Are you engaged to Maine after knowing him just one day?"

"No, of course not. He's trying—that is, it's his way of protecting me, I guess." Though that wasn't the way Maine had put it. He had said, "protecting my interests." And it was not mine he had meant.

"You seem," Arthur commented in some amusement, "to have acquired a number of protectors. I appear to have underestimated Maine's enterprise and his capacity for prompt action. And Knight, too! He comes rushing to the rescue just because the telephone is out of order. As it happens, Knight, we were discussing you just before you arrived. You seem to be in the unfortunate position of being the only one without an

alibi for the murder of that chap—what's his name?—
Cooper."

Ken was very still, only his eyes moving from face
to face.

"No," I intervened, "Maine has no alibi. He was
sick and he didn't stay for the funeral. Were the rest of
you together the whole time?"

"This is intolerable," Nell said. "Dad and I were
together, weren't we?"

Guthrie nodded emphatically. "Of course. Every
single minute."

"How about you, Arthur?"

"I drove my own car, of course, but I joined Nell
and Mr. Harcourt at the church and followed them
back from the cemetery."

"What about the Wenskis?" I asked.

Maine looked at me soberly. "You're determined to
clear Ken Knight, aren't you?"

"He didn't get here until after I found the body."

With a shrug, Maine went out to the kitchen and
then I heard him tap on the door of the studio. He
returned in a few minutes to say, "Dr. Graves gave
them a lift to the church. Then he had to see a patient,
so he couldn't take them to the cemetery. Someone
picked them up. Then Sonia got a lift back, but
Leopold had to walk."

Ken had tossed his topcoat on a chair. He pulled a
pipe out of his pocket and began to fill it, tamping
down the tobacco, watching all of us.

"You are a loyal young woman," Arthur told me.
"And, I might add, a very trusting one."

When I made no comment he went on in that warm
flexible voice that must have a terrific impact on a jury,
"This is no time for finesse. We have one overwhelming fact to face. Apparently the man Cooper was hired

to kill you to prevent you from inheriting the Harcourt estate. But only one person knew about that will. Kendrick Knight."

"Sonia Wenski knew. She told me so this afternoon. And, what's more, she told someone else."

"Who?"

"She refused to say, but she'll have to tell the police."

The fire had burned down in the grate and there was no light in the room but the flickering candles. As the glow from the fireplace faded, it was impossible to read expressions. Within a few minutes it became difficult even to make out where people were sitting or standing.

A vine growing against the north window rattled sharply in the wind and I must have jumped a foot. "Aren't there any more candles? Isn't there a lantern or a flashlight or something."

"Steady." Ken was somehow beside me; his hand slipped under my arm.

Guthrie blundered through the room and knocked against a table, setting a candlestick rocking. Nell had changed position; I could smell her perfume as she moved.

Then Ken released me and moved away. The wind rose to a scream and there was a gust of cold air. The heavy draperies that had been drawn over the north window belled out as though someone had moved behind them and then fell into place again. The doorbell rang.

There was the rustling of paper as Sonia came through the room, carrying a candle which she held well away from her inflammable costume. She opened the door and then stepped back, sheltering the flame. I saw the masked figure in the doorway, saw the gleam

111

of the knife, and then the candle went out and the door slammed shut.

There was a frozen moment and then a crash as Sonia fell to the floor. Maine caught up a branched candlestick and came to look down at her.

"My God! She's been hurt."

Arthur pushed past him, knelt beside the girl. There was a queer rattle in her throat and then nothing at all. He put down the hand he was holding, laying it gently on the rug. "She's gone," he said blankly. "She's dead."

Guthrie blundered toward them and Maine pulled him away.

"What killed her?" Ken asked.

"She must have been stabbed. There was no shot, and there's a lot of blood."

"Is the knife there?"

"Why, no. He must have taken it with him."

"You mean," Maine said incredulously, "that it was an outsider?"

"Good God! What did you think, man? Didn't you see him in the doorway?"

"We'll have to get Dr. Graves," Guthrie said.

"But the girl has been murdered," Arthur told him. "One of us will have to go for the police."

And at that Nell began to scream shrilly and horribly.

10

Unexpectedly and blindingly the lights came on. The furnace thumped reassuringly. The refrigerator began to hum. The house was alive again and we were once more linked by telephone with the outside world.

For a moment we stood blinking in the light, and then we all turned to look at the crumpled figure with its absurd mask and the paper costume with the horrible red stain. The blood was still wet and glistening, but it did not spread. My first feeling was a dull surprise that she had been so much smaller than I had realized.

I reached out to remove the mask, which was not funny now, which was ugly and obscene and made a mockery of death. Arthur caught my hand. "You mustn't touch anything, you know."

"Just the mask. I can't bear it."

"Steady. Maine, I'll call the police. For God's sake, try to control Nell! No, damn it, Harcourt! You can't have a drink now. You've got to pull yourself together before you're asked any questions. Knight, you had better let Leopold know what has happened."

Arthur had taken complete charge easily and quickly, and nobody refused to obey his curt orders. Guthrie, who had been on his way to the liquor supply in the dining room, stopped short and came back. He sat down in the nook behind the stairs, where he could not see the small still figure on the rug.

Maine had reached Nell's side. "Stop it!" he told her sharply. She ignored him, continuing to scream. He shook her and then slapped her cheek. She caught her breath then and began to sob, her whole body shaking, but at least the hysterics were at an end. Ken, after a long look at me, went out to the kitchen and through the door to the studio.

I don't believe I thought at all. My heart seemed to be tumbling over and over and I could not stop shaking, but I did not think. Murder had been done before my eyes, before the eyes of six people, and the murderer had simply closed the door behind him and gone out into the night, had melted into the darkness.

It may have been a minute or five minutes before Leopold flung open the kitchen door and ran across the dining room. He shoved me out of his way, but I don't believe he was aware of that. He knelt down beside the quiet little figure.

"Don't touch her," I warned him as he reached instinctively to remove that grotesque mask.

"God, I'm going to be sick," Nell said, and Maine steered her down the passage to the powder room.

"I have a right," Leopold said. "She's my wife."

"But you may be destroying evidence," I told him. The musician's ugly hand paused on that sodden paper costume, dropped away. He looked up at me then. There was a moment before he grasped the implication of what I had said.

"I won't destroy any clues," he said roughly. "One of you killed her and I intend to find out who it was."

"My dear boy," Guthrie expostulated. He came to lay a pudgy hand on Leopold's sleeve. "She was stabbed by an outsider. She opened the door, a masked man stabbed her, and then he got away."

"Take your filthy paws off me!" Leopold said. "Masked man! What kind of soap opera—"

"Trick or Treat night," I reminded him. "Someone took advantage of it."

"Yeah." Leopold was standing now. "Anyone think to call the police?"

Arthur had come back to join us. "I called them." As Nell returned to the room, dead white, Maine holding her arm, Arthur eased her into a chair. "Better now?"

She nodded without looking at him, her head resting on the back of the chair, her eyes closed. She drew away slightly from his touch.

"I've got to have a drink," Guthrie muttered.

"Better not," Maine said. "What we need is some coffee." He glanced toward Leopold, who had not moved from his position beside his wife's body, as though anything could hurt her now. "Nell, will you fix it?"

"If you need coffee, you can make it yourself. Or ask the new lady of the house. Let Cathy do it."

Anything was better than sitting there and shaking. I got up. "I'll make it."

In the kitchen, which Sonia had left clean and shining, I found coffee, the drip pot, cups and saucers. When a hand touched me, I nearly screamed.

"Sorry," Ken said, "I thought you saw me."

"Will he get away?"

"He?"

"The murderer, of course."

"But, Cathy, she was killed by someone inside the living room."

115

"That's impossible. I saw him. I tell you I saw it with my own eyes."

"Exactly what did you see? Exactly what happened? Remember how dark it was in the room, how unexpectedly the thing happened."

"The wind came up and blew out the draperies. Then the doorbell rang and Sonia came to open the door. I saw a man wearing a mask by the light of her candle, and the gleam of the knife. Then the wind blew out the candle she was holding, the door closed, and she fell."

"You still don't get it, do you?"

"What do you mean?"

"That wind before the bell rang. Someone from inside opened the door, rang the bell, waited to be seen, blew out Sonia's candle, and closed the door. *But he was still inside*. In the darkness you couldn't tell where anyone was. No one could tell. Leopold was right. It was one of us."

"But if it was one of us, what happened to the mask and the knife? There was no time to hide them."

I filled cups and Ken carried the tray through the dining room, where Guthrie was taking a quick drink, and into the living room, where he served the coffee.

"How about you?" he asked Leopold.

The latter hesitated. "Okay," he said dully. "I guess I might as well."

When car lights moved toward the house, Nell went to clutch at Arthur's sleeve. "Oh, God," she whispered. "Oh, God."

"It will be all right." Of us all he was the only one who had retained full self-possession. "Think before you speak. Don't volunteer anything. Don't answer if I tell you not to. Can you manage that, Nell?"

116

Her eyes, wide and blank, looked at him without comprehension, but she nodded obediently.

Arthur looked around. "That applies to all of you, of course."

"Like hell it does," Leopold said. "I'm not covering up for anybody. Not anybody. Someone stabbed my wife, and I intend to find out who did it. No smart lawyer is going to cover up a thing."

Maine opened the door and, because we were all more or less braced to face the police, it was a letdown when Dr. Graves came into the room. He stood stock-still as he looked at the figure in the grotesque mask.

"Good God! Poor Cathy!"

And then Nell went off into a peal of laughter. It was to the sound of that uncontrolled laughter that Maine opened the door a second time and admitted Captain Grieg and Sergeant Mendelssohn.

II

Captain Grieg had abandoned his fatherly manner, and it was a grim man who came to us at length in the dining room into which we had been herded while pictures were taken and men worked swiftly and quietly.

When the mask with its great beaked nose was removed at last, Grieg said sharply, "How did this happen?"

Arthur, who had been watching proceedings from the dining room door—the rest of us had been careful not to look—said, "That bruise on her face? Oh, her husband did that. They had a quarrel this evening and he struck her. We all heard it."

Leopold, who sat humped in a chair, his elbows on

the dining room table and his face buried in his hands, sat up with a jerk. "That—" he began abruptly and then he fell silent.

"Perhaps you'd like to explain," Grieg suggested.

"My wife was stabbed to death when I was in the studio. I'm the only one of the lot who could not have killed her. If these people aren't all liars, they will bear me out in that."

"He's the only one who was not in the room when she was killed," I agreed. "Anyhow, I thought the man came from outside. I saw him at the door."

Again Ken advanced his theory that the killer had opened the door to ring, let himself be seen in a mask, and then stepped inside and closed the door after him.

While the police experimented, opening the door, observing the way the curtain billowed out, Arthur commented. "Knight seems to be hell-bent on causing trouble for us."

"He has some fanciful ideas. I've noticed that," Grieg admitted.

"You forget," Ken said, "the place was as dark as hell, we could barely see each other except as shadows until after the electricity came back on. Anyone could have opened the door unseen, and there's no other way of accounting for the way the draperies billowed out. And I don't agree that this eliminates even Leopold. He could have been in the room and we would have been most unlikely to notice him."

"I'd never have killed my wife," Leopold said. "Never."

"But you struck her."

"Okay, I slapped her. She was getting out of line and just asking for trouble."

"What kind of trouble?" Grieg asked alertly.

"The kind she got."

"How was she doing that?"

When Leopold was silent, I said, "Blackmail."

"Cathy!" Arthur protested.

"She doesn't mean it," Maine said. "Cathy is terribly upset, probably in shock. She doesn't mean it."

"I do too mean it. That's what Sonia was getting at when we were having dinner and she said she intended to make a fortune."

Ken looked as though he wanted to strangle me. Arthur was worried and determined to stop me from making more of a fool of myself.

"My dear girl," Guthrie expostulated, his fat fingers covering my hand. "My dear girl. There's no reason on earth for Sonia to attempt to blackmail any of us."

"She told someone that I was to be Aunt Geraldine's heir. And tonight she was shouting at her husband something about the fact that he couldn't make her keep still, that no one could."

Dr. Graves had come into the dining room to join us after completing his examination of the body.

He caught Grieg's eyes and nodded. "You can take her away now. In the morning I'll—" He saw Leopold watching him and checked what he was going to say.

While Grieg sent Mendelssohn to give orders, Dr. Graves came to put his fingers on my pulse. "I'll leave you some sleeping pills for tonight."

Arthur indicated Nell. "I think Mrs. Glenn needs something. She's been greatly upset."

Grieg had turned to Leopold. "Do you know of any reason why your wife would blackmail anyone?"

"She knew something, but she wouldn't tell me what it was. Something about the shadows."

"Shadows!" Grieg exclaimed in surprise.

Leopold nodded. "Something she thought was kind of funny, a practical joke of some sort."

119

"But there was no one about whom she seemed to have some secret knowledge?"

There was a moment of hesitation and then, slowly and helplessly, the color flooded into Leopold's face. At last it ebbed and he shook his head. "No one."

"She was your own wife," I sputtered angrily. "Are you trying to protect her killer?"

"Cathy," Arthur warned me, "you really must not volunteer comments of that kind."

"Miss Briggs is right and you're wrong," Leopold said. "It was just—well, my wife is—she was kind of jealous—and Mrs. Glenn—well, now and then she had me go to her room to fix the taps in the bathroom or to do some odd job or something like that—"

"Really," Nell said, "of all the ridiculous ideas. Jealous of me!" And then she made a mistake. "A servant!"

This time Leopold's eyes were hard and bright. "Or a truck driver or a guy behind the counter at a diner or the milkman or—"

"Cut it out," Maine said. "I am willing to make a lot of allowances for you but, damn it, man, she's my sister. Cut it out!"

"Okay, okay." Leopold shrugged elaborately.

Grieg gave crisp orders and a man came to set up his apparatus on the dining room table and take our fingerprints. Only Leopold balked and then submitted with a fatalistic air. When this had been done, the captain called the men into the kitchen, one at a time, to be searched. Neither the knife nor the mask was found. In the living room, men were prodding chairs and looking under couches.

At last Grieg said, "I'll have to have the two young ladies searched, too. I can take you in and have a police matron do it or you can search each other."

So Nell and I withdrew to the kitchen. In a way it was a ridiculous performance. It would have been impossible for Nell to conceal anything but a handkerchief in that scanty evening dress, but I went through the gestures. She did a thorough job on me. We didn't exchange a word until we were ready to rejoin the others.

"Take my advice, Cathy," Nell said. "Marry Maine as soon as you can. That's your only chance."

When we had returned to the dining room, Grieg left a trooper to watch us and took a couple of men to search the big studio. Leopold wasn't interested. There was a little bustle in the living room and he stood watching while his wife's small body was carried out of the room. His face was somber. I did not think that he had loved her, at least not with the possessive, obsessive love she had had for him, but I believed that he had been fond of her and grateful for her adoration. When the door had closed and a car started up, he turned to stare at Nell. For the first time he noticed the pearl necklace.

"You're wearing Mrs. Harcourt's necklace," he said. "I'd be willing to bet my last dollar she didn't give it to you."

Nell's fingers closed over it convulsively and her eyes were frightened. Leopold looked at me. "These people took a real beating when you raked in the whole jackpot. From more than a million apiece to twenty-five thousand. You watch yourself, lady. Sonia got in the way and look what happened to her. So you—"

"One more word out of you," Arthur began furiously, and Leopold subsided.

Dr. Graves said, "My dear, I don't think we should take any chance on you. Why don't you come back to my house for a while? I have a housekeeper who can make you comfortable and a part-time gardener and handyman who can stay on guard in the house, day and night, as long as it is necessary."

"Cathy will be safe in this house, Doctor," Guthrie said with more dignity than I would have expected. "Any suggestion that one of us would injure her is monstrous."

"Ken Knight and I had dinner together this evening," the doctor said. "I had heard a rumor from my office girl that Cathy was to marry Maine Harcourt. We were discussing Mrs. Harcourt's death in the light of subsequent events. I must admit that I am no longer sure it was an accident."

"Arthur," Guthrie said, "are there grounds for a suit against Graves? I do not intend to remain quiet while my children and myself are practically accused of murder." He was almost physically puffed up with indignation or what passed for indignation. But I remembered our walk along the millstream, the increasing pressure of his hand, the way he had steered me closer and closer to that slippery bank and the drop below. Suppose Maine had not come racing toward us, shouting my name, just when he did?

"At least," Ken said, his voice expressionless, "if anything, however accidental it might appear, should happen to Cathy while she is at the mill—"

"Nothing will happen to her," Maine said. "You have my personal assurance on that point."

At Arthur's suggestion, the trooper who had been left to guard us and who had been standing, taking in every word, sat down. Guthrie's head gradually dropped on his chest and he began to snore. Nell had moved close to Arthur and slipped her hand under his arm. Maine stood behind my chair, his hands resting lightly on my shoulders. I could see his face in a mirror over the buffet. Of them all, he looked the worst—haggard, drawn, his eyes too bright.

Dr. Graves left me some sleeping pills and took his departure. Ken and Arthur faced each other across the table and once more their enmity and distrust was almost tangible. Whatever the cause of their bitterness, it must, I thought, lie somewhere in the past, and it had something to do with the death of Ken's wife in the millstream. The disturbing factor was that Ken had profited by that death; it had, apparently, made him a rich man.

Leopold sat watching Nell with an unnerving steadiness. It was an altogether silent tableau into which Captain Grieg stepped when he came through from the kitchen, followed by several men. During that long wait we had been aware that pictures were being taken, that the room was being searched.

Grieg looked at all of us. Then his hand moved swiftly. "Do any of you recognize this?" Hanging from a string looped around the handle was a hunting knife, the blade stained red.

At the sound of his sharp question, Guthrie awakened with a startled snort and sat upright. For a long moment we all stared at the stained knife.

"Is that what—did it?" Leopold asked at last.

"It seems to be. Is it yours?"

"I never saw it before."

Each of us in turn looked at it in a kind of morbid fascination and shook our heads.

"You found that in our room?" Leopold demanded, and for the first time there was more than anger and defiance in his voice; there was fear.

"Under the mattress on the studio couch."

"I swear to God I didn't put it there. I'm being framed. I didn't kill her. I'd never have killed her."

Grieg nodded to one of the men who held out a small black mask. "Found this under the lid of the grand piano."

"Then it must have been an outsider, after all," Maine exclaimed in a combination of surprise and relief. "None of us had an opportunity to plant these things in Leopold's room."

11

"Actually," Ken said, "every single one of us could have planted the knife and mask in the studio."

"How do you make that out?" Arthur asked.

"Let's start with you. While you telephoned the police, you were out of our sight for minutes. Nell was sick and Maine steered her back past the studio door to the powder room. They were both gone anywhere from five to ten minutes. Harcourt went into the dining room to get a drink. I went into the studio to tell Leopold about his wife. After he came out, Cathy was in the kitchen making coffee."

"We found something else," Grieg said, and one of the troopers held out a handful of bills. "Two hundred dollars. People don't often have that much lying around in cash."

"Mrs. Harcourt gave it to us, a hundred each to Sonia and me, when we witnessed her will," Leopold said.

"It isn't necessary or customary to pay witnesses," Arthur commented.

"Mrs. Harcourt was like that; she sort of looked for excuses to give us some money now and then, so we wouldn't feel too heavily obligated to her. She knew that even if I should get rave reviews when I appear at Town Hall, there will be some lean times while I am getting set, getting recital dates, all that."

"I can vouch for that," Ken said. "I was there when Mrs. Harcourt gave them the money."

"In fact," Nell said, "anything that touches on that second will you'll vouch for."

Arthur shook his head at her and she fell silent.

"Wasn't it bad enough, for God's sake, to stab my wife without trying to throw the blame on me?" Leopold exclaimed.

"The queer thing is," Grieg commented, "that while the knife was hidden in your room, there are no fingerprints on it."

"Which makes no sense at all," Arthur said.

"Which makes a great deal of sense," Grieg replied. "The killer's chief need was to get rid of the knife and the mask." He turned to Mendelssohn. "Let's see how that stuff works."

Mendelssohn had a package wrapped in newspaper. He opened it carefully. Inside there was a quantity of black crepe, the kind that is used for widows' mourning veils. He spread it out. There must have been yards and yards of the stuff, and it seemed to be oddly packed until I realized that it was wired.

"What the hell is that?" Leopold demanded.

"That is what I am asking you," the captain said.

"I never saw it before."

"It was in your wife's half of the clothes closet, behind the big cellophane bag that holds her winter coat."

"What's it for?"

Grieg looked at Nell but there was nothing to be read in her face beyond the same bewilderment we all felt. "I have a kind of idea that this is the explanation for the shadows that so disturbed Mrs. Harcourt."

For a few moments Mendelssohn experimented until he was able to cause a flicker of darkness behind a chair, or in one of the many nooks of the room.

"What a filthy thing to do!" I exploded.

"It's my idea," Grieg said, "that Sonia was creating the shadows." As Leopold started to protest, he stopped him with a peremptory gesture. "I don't think she realized all the implications because she seemed to be genuinely grateful to Mrs. Harcourt for what she was doing for you. From what I've seen of her, she was like a child and it was probably a game to her."

"But not to Aunt Geraldine," I said. "She was frightened."

"I think that's what it was meant to do—drive her into doubting her own mental stability. Well," Grieg nodded and Mendelssohn began to repack the black crepe, "there won't be any more shadows in the mill. I can guarantee that."

"There were shadows in the mill when I got here," I said. "That's what disturbed me and made me go outside where I found that man."

Apparently Leopold had accepted the likelihood of his wife's culpability. "She got a lift home from the cemetery and I had to walk. I guess maybe—but the kid didn't mean any harm."

"But when she understood about the wills and their implications," Grieg pointed out, "she knew what had been going on and she intended to put a bite on."

"It would have been for my sake," Leopold said awkwardly. "She didn't really want anything for herself."

To my surprise Grieg put his hand on the bereaved young husband's shoulder in a gesture that was almost

127

fatherly. "No one is blaming her. Okay, kid, take it easy. But we want to find the one who killed her, don't we?"

"Yes." The boy's tone was almost savage.

"Just remember, son, that if she was here in the mill, the chances are a hundred to one she saw the murderer, even if she didn't know at the time what was going on. Who brought your wife back here from the cemetery?"

"I don't know." Leopold saw the doubting expression. "I'm not afraid to tell you. By God, if I knew I'd be shouting it. But I swear to God, sir, I don't know. She just told me she had a lift and I stayed behind a few minutes to help arrange the flowers."

Grieg looked around. It was nearly two o'clock. "That's all for tonight. I don't want anyone leaving town without informing me. I'll talk to you all again tomorrow. And I'm leaving a man on guard here tonight. We're going to have to seal the studio. Wenski, I don't want you to leave. Have you a place to sleep?"

Maine shrugged. "He can use a couch, I suppose."

Arthur came to take my hand in both of his. "I'll see you tomorrow. Sleep well. If you need me for anything, I'll come at once." He turned to put his arm around Nell. "You're dead on your feet. Ask Cathy for one of her sleeping pills. Take care of yourself." He nodded to the other men and went out.

Ken came straight to me, lifted my chin, and to my amazement, he kissed me on the mouth. "My seal." Without another word he went out and I heard his motor race before he moved away.

That was a horrible night. We stumbled up the stairs, Maine white and angry, holding my arm; Nell seeming to be half dazed. Guthrie went back to the dining room for a final nightcap and I heard him exchange a few words with the trooper who had been left on guard, suggesting that he get some sleep on one of the couches in the living room.

Before going into my own room, I turned to Nell. "Dr. Graves left me four sleeping pills. Don't you want to take two of them?"

"I'm not going to let myself be knocked out," Nell said. She went into her room, banged the door behind her, and then the key turned in the lock. The bedsprings protested as she appeared to throw herself full length on the bed. She began to cry, loud, unrestrained crying, like that of a small child.

As I started to knock on her door, Maine caught my hand. "Let her alone, Cathy. She'll be better off by herself. Anything you could do or say would only make things worse, feeling as she does about you. You'll be all right, you know. I'll keep my door open so—" He drew me into his arms. "I'll look out for you." When I tried to release myself, his arms tightened. "Cathy, I meant it, you know, when I asked you to marry me. That would solve everything."

"Stop that, Maine, and let me go at once."

He still held me, one arm like an iron band across my shoulders. With his free hand he lifted my chin. I turned my head sharply to one side.

"You let Knight kiss you." Maine's pleasant voice roughened. "Was that his price for the second will?"

"Good night," Guthrie called cheerfully to the trooper as he started up the stairs.

Maine released me. His face had changed in the past few hours; it had grown older and its air of gentleness was gone.

Guthrie, coming up from the landing, beamed at us both. "Sorry to disturb you."

"You didn't disturb me. Good night." I went quickly into Aunt Geraldine's room, locked the door, and then hauled up a straight chair and jammed the back under the handle of the door. I undressed quickly, opened the window and then, because of the force of the wind, pulled it down, leaving only a crack. I poured water and started to take two of the sleeping pills and then put them down uncertainly. I'd have liked to blot everything out, but part of me wanted to keep on guard.

I got into bed and switched out the light. Almost immediately I switched it on again, listening to the howling of the wind, to the sudden snapping of a branch in the storm, to the rush of water in the millstream, to the house itself, creaking and protesting against the force of the wind.

There was a clock with a radium dial beside the bed and I watched the second hand race around, saw the hour hand creep, waiting for morning and the reassurance of daylight.

For a long time I could hear Nell's racking sobs; then they subsided into softer hiccuping sounds and I thought she had gone to sleep. But she was walking up and down her room, up and down, up and down, the beat of her feet a staccato counterpoint to the slow, steady sound of the trooper making his rounds. Once he apparently threw a log on the fire and I nearly leaped out of bed.

I tried counting and reciting poetry and recalling the exact position of every object in the room at my boarding house, trying to drive out the intolerable pictures in my mind: Sonia wearing that grotesque mask, the gleam of a knife, the swift movement of the man in the mask, the closing door. Had he gone out or had he remained inside? After the candle had been blown out, I hadn't seen anything.

What kind of person was this killer who had—and I felt sure of it now—killed Aunt Geraldine, killed Tim Cooper, killed Sonia?

I remembered what Arthur had said about some places seeming to attract violence, as the mill had done. That horrible Maybury slaying, Ken Knight's wife lying in the deep place in the millstream; Tim Cooper with his foot caught, lying on his face with the water rippling cheerfully over him; Aunt Geraldine crumpled on the landing with a broken neck; Sonia in the witch's costume, the paper soaked with her blood.

The staccato sound of Nell's high heels beat on; below there was the heavier pounding of the trooper's tread, the wind made the curtains billow out into the room and fall again. I turned over on my face, trying to muffle the sounds with my pillow, and then I was afraid of things behind me and turned back to reassure myself by looking around the room. I could see every inch of it clearly. I knew the bathroom and closet were empty.

I began to attempt to sort out my thoughts. Aunt Geraldine had been killed for her estate. Who would profit by her death? If—as had been expected—I had been safely dead by the time her body was found, the money would have gone to Guthrie, Nell, and Maine. Guthrie was drowning his anxieties in the only way he knew how, through drinking himself into a stupor. Nell had gone to pieces, as though her nerves had reached their snapping point. Maine was determined to force me to marry him. Why? To insure getting at least a part of the estate or to prevent either his father or his sister from making any further attempts on my life?

I was startled to realize that I could consider the possibility of one of them being the killer without doing any violence to my own reason. Was Maine afraid for them or for me or for himself? I couldn't even guess which one it was. That he was attracted to me I was well aware, but I doubted whether that had much to do with his determination to marry me. Certainly that would please Guthrie. And Nell had said it was my only chance.

Then a new thought struck me. Aunt Geraldine's death and Tim Cooper's and Sonia Wenski's—there was a common denominator—the Harcourt estate. But what about the death of Ken Knight's wife in the millstream? What accounted for the deep enmity between Arthur and Ken? She had left her money, "a packet," to Ken. He had been on the scene shortly after I reached the mill; he could, I saw now, have been there before I arrived. He had rushed to the mill when he heard the rumor that I was engaged to Maine, as though that had thrown off his calculations in some way.

Something moved outside my door and I sat bolt upright, holding my breath. For a moment someone stood so close to the door I heard the sound of cloth brushing against it. Then there were firm footsteps on the stairs as the trooper started up, and the footsteps moved hastily away, someone walking without shoes.

There was a faint tap on my door and I said, "Who's there?"

"Trooper Gray, miss." He kept his voice low. "Saw your light. I just wanted to be sure you're okay."

"Thank you, Trooper. Good night."

"Good night, miss."

I was in safe hands. Nothing would happen. In my relief I reached out to switch off the lights, turned on my side, and fell sound asleep.

III

It was the sound of my own name that awakened me. I blinked sleep-filled eyes and saw that it was nine-thirty. I had slept almost four hours.

"It's Cathy's house. Let her do the work. Or do it yourself." That was Nell's voice, shrill and too high-pitched.

I took a hasty shower and put on the black dress. Today I'd have to buy at least sweaters and skirts. When I ran downstairs, a trooper, whom I had not seen the night before, gave me a swift look. "You Miss Briggs?"

I nodded.

"Trooper Williams. Captain Grieg said to tell you the inquest on Cooper will be at eleven. You'll have time for breakfast first." He added, "I guess."

I thought his expression was rather odd and I knew why when I went into the kitchen. Leopold was sitting at the kitchen table drinking coffee and eating a scrambled egg on toast. He had prepared only enough for one and Nell, who looked ravaged, with dark smears of fatigue under her eyes, which were red-rimmed and swollen, and her skin like putty, was snapping at him.

Maine and Guthrie hovered around, looking helpless and annoyed.

"Out," I told them. "I'll get breakfast. Just get out of my way."

Nell and her father went out; Maine turned toward

133

me with a purposeful air. I held him off with one hand. "If you want anything to eat, go away."

When he had gone, Leopold, to my surprise, got up, cleared away his dishes, and made fresh coffee. "I'll fix your breakfast, Miss Briggs."

"Thank you." Impulsively I held out my hand. "I didn't have a chance last night—I'm terribly sorry. Terribly."

His handclasp was firm. "Poor little fool," he said, but not ungently. "She was playing in the big league and she didn't know it, she didn't know what she was tangled with until it was too late. Then all she knew how to do was to hand out a lot of clumsy warnings. If she had only told me! And the hell of it was that she did it for me. She must have been promised some money and she didn't want anything for herself. Just for me."

"Have you any idea which one it is?" I asked.

He started to speak, and changed his mind.

"Please tell me, if you know."

"I don't know for sure."

"But you suspect—"

"That's not healthy around here. I'd clear out this morning except that I don't want to lose that studio, not until I've made my debut. I've got to have a place to practice."

"But can't you tell the police what you suspect?"

"If the murderer knows what I think I know, I wouldn't give five cents for my life. The stake isn't peanuts, Miss Briggs."

He poured coffee and put a plate of scrambled eggs and toast in front of me.

"Thank you, but what about the others?"

He shrugged. "That's their lookout. They can go to

the drugstore in the village. They've still got their health."

There was no point in arguing with him, and I couldn't blame him when he believed that one of them had murdered his wife.

"I don't suppose there's a newspaper in town."

"Only Mr. Knight's weekly. But you'd better brace yourself, Miss Briggs. The story is out—and how! It's been on the radio, not only the local station but the national. Probably on television by this time, only Mrs. Harcourt didn't have a television set. And men have been telephoning from the newspapers since five o'clock this morning. Kept the trooper busy answering the telephone."

"What did he tell them?"

"Nothing, but as he said 'Trooper Gray speaking' when he answered, that was enough to set them off. They'll be at the inquest and probably there are a dozen newsmen and cameramen flying up from New York and over from Boston."

"It was a horrible thing to happen to your wife, but I don't see why the story should interest anyone out of Milltown."

Leopold cocked an eyebrow and switched on the radio. "Local station," he explained. "They've gone haywire. They've already had an interview with an expert on poltergeists and haunted houses and witchcraft—"

The tubes had warmed up. "For those who have tuned in late, murder once more stalks the Old Mill at Milltown. Last night a mysterious masked killer stabbed to death the young wife of a concert pianist, Leopold Wenski, at the famous building renovated by the late Mrs. Harcourt. The murder victim, wearing a witch's costume, was apparently taking part in some Halloween rite.

"Only two days ago, the body of a murdered man was found in the millstream by Mrs. Harcourt's niece, Miss Catherine Briggs, who arrived in Milltown too late to attend her aunt's funeral. It is now alleged that Mrs. Harcourt's death may not have been accidental as was at first reported. The lovely young woman, who is said to be her aunt's heiress, has spent an eventful two days since she reached Milltown. She not only found a dead body and witnessed a young woman's murder and acquired a great fortune, but she has been involved in a whirlwind courtship and she is expected to marry Maine Harcourt, nephew of the late Gerald Harcourt.

"To recapitulate the history of the Old Mill, tragedy first struck it some thirty years ago when a drunken miller . . . "

With a sardonic look at me, Leopold switched it off. "Thought maybe you'd had enough, but it gives you a rough idea."

I pushed away my plate. "They make it sound as though Maine Harcourt and I had gone on a murdering spree."

The doorbell rang and I started. "You've about had it," Leopold said. "You just stay here and drink another cup of coffee."

Evidently the trooper opened the door. None of the Harcourts would think of exerting themselves. I heard Arthur Mattheson's beautiful, carrying voice. "Cathy here?"

"In the kitchen getting breakfast," Maine said. "Good morning, Doctor."

"I brought Dr. Graves along to see whether you are all in shape for the inquest."

136

"What are we supposed to do?" Guthrie asked. "You'll brief us, won't you?"

"Well, it's really Cathy they'll want to question, because she found the body. The rest of you need only say you never saw the man before and, if they ask, tell them your alibis for the time of the murder. Now if Cathy—"

"She's got Maine right where she wants him, hasn't she?" Nell said. "She's got Ken Knight. Does she have to—" Her voice began to rise and unexpectedly she started to scream—horrible screams that tore holes in the fabric of the room like a sonic boom.

"All right," Dr. Graves said quietly. "Just roll up your sleeve, Mrs. Glenn. That's right."

"What are you doing?"

"Putting you under sedation."

"No! No! I'm not going to be unconscious. I've got to be able to protect myself."

"Help her up to her room, will you, Maine?" Dr. Graves said. "She should be asleep in a few minutes."

"No! No!"

I covered my ears, trying to shut out the cry. Then the trooper said, "All right, ma'am. I'll just take your arm. I'll be outside your door. You're quite safe, ma'am."

I heard their steps on the stairs, the trooper's heavy and firm, Nell's shuffling. Then there was blessed quiet.

I lifted my head and was surprised to see how ugly Leopold's expression was. "Sure nice to be a dame and be able to pull hysterics if you want to avoid an inquest."

I stared at him. "You think Mrs. Glenn was faking?"

He was embarrassed but dogged. "Look, anyone can tell what she's like. Can't help the way she's

137

made, maybe, only she got Sonia sore, and Sonia knew something about her, I mean something more than—" He tried again. "She's the only one who ever fought with Sonia. And she's bad medicine. She hates your guts, Miss Briggs; I'm warning you right now."

"Why?"

"Not just because you're a rival she can't beat on looks, but it's the money. Well, look at it this way. Old Harcourt maybe isn't too worried, because he has always had someone to pick up the tab for him; he thinks someone always will. Maine—well, if he can marry you, he has it made. But Mrs. Glenn—she's been around too long, too often. If she's going to get a man and keep him, she has to have something more to offer, a lot more. Yeah, she's the big loser in this game."

He stopped as the kitchen door swung open and Maine came out.

He gave a hopeful look to see whether there was any breakfast, accepted the inevitable in good part. "Ready, Cathy?"

"Yes, I'm ready."

"Arthur wants a word before you go. So do I." He gave me a cool kiss on the cheek. "Sorry about last night. Guess I was rushing things."

12

There was a crowd outside the building where the inquest was to be held, and Maine, who had driven Guthrie and me in the Cadillac, had difficulty in finding a place, nearly two blocks away, in which to park. As a result, we had to walk back, facing a barrage of cameramen and reporters, as well as the eyes of curious bystanders.

Later I saw some of the pictures. One of them in particular I remember. I was standing between Maine and Guthrie like a prisoner between two jailers.

"Miss Briggs! . . . Hey, look this way, Miss Briggs. . . . Is it true you're going to marry young Harcourt? . . . What's the truth about the masked man? . . . Is the Old Mill haunted? . . . Was the murdered woman a witch? . . . How'd you happen to find that body in the millstream? . . . Miss Briggs, the *Sentinel* would like a five-thousand word story of your life. We'd do the work and all you'd—"

And then I heard the ugliest sound from the crowd that had in some way become a mob. A boo. I shrank as though I had received a physical blow.

Arthur Mattheson came charging through the crowd, brushing them aside as though they were flies. He took me away from the two Harcourt men, muttering his opinion of them for failing to protect me in a low voice but words that must have scorched.

His hand on my arm steadied me. I hadn't been

prepared for the publicity and the curiosity, and I was shaking.

"It's going to be all right," he assured me. "Don't rush anything. Take your time. All we want today is an open verdict. This isn't a trial, you know. They're just going to ask how you happened to find the body. It will be over almost before you know it. I've had a talk with the coroner."

But Arthur hadn't counted on the advance job the reporters had done. The coroner was willing to keep the proceedings short, but the men and women who had been called upon to serve as a jury were not so easily satisfied. Nor were the spectators who filled the little room. They must all have heard the broadcasts and there wasn't, it seemed to me, a single person in the place who looked at me without suspicion or even open hostility, though why they thought I would have killed Tim Cooper, I couldn't imagine. A good deal of that hostility, of course, had been stirred up by the statement that I had become engaged to Maine practically the minute I met him, though in all fairness they should have held that more against Maine than against me. Whether I was supposed to be buying a husband or silencing an enemy, I didn't know.

Captain Grieg identified the dead man as Tim Cooper from fingerprints on record and what they called mug shots. There was a cocky-looking young man on the jury, the kind who goes through life suspecting that people are trying to put something over on him and is determined to protect his own rights. Before Captain Grieg could leave the stand, the young juryman demanded to know why the mug shots and fingerprints were on file. The captain, annoyed, answered briefly that the man had been in the hands of the police before.

Oh, so he had a criminal record, the brash young man said alertly. And what was a man like that doing at the Old Mill?

He was not at the Old Mill; he was in the millstream. And it was not the purpose of this inquiry to determine the reason for the man's presence, only to decide whether or not he had been murdered.

The captain left the witness stand and Dr. Graves described his examination of the body. The brash young man, whose name, it appeared, was Smith, had tasted blood. "The members of the jury would like to know, Doctor," he said before the coroner could stop him, "whether there's any doubt in your mind that the man was murdered? A lump behind his ear inflicted by a blunt instrument, water in his lungs, he had been searched before he went into the millstream. Right?"

"That is correct," Dr. Graves said.

"Could it have been some sort of queer religious or superstitious rite like last night's killing?"

"That's out of line, young man," the coroner said swiftly. "This court is concerned only with the death of Tim Cooper."

Smith was not so easily silenced. Probably he had never before experienced the intoxication of having a captive audience. "But you can't deny there is some connection between the two murders."

The coroner's small hammer pounded on the table. It was a very angry man who looked along the lines of faces in the jury box. "You will forget that any such outrageous statement was made," he directed. When he looked at Smith, the young man quailed, though I think he was rather pleased with himself, too. For days to come he would be buttonholing people and saying, "And so I told them—"

When I was called, I took a long breath and then

141

walked swiftly up to the chair, looking straight ahead of me. They're only a pack of cards, I told myself firmly. Only a pack of cards. I made myself look at the faces in the room, not a large room and, at the moment, every seat was filled and people were crowded against the wall. At first in my panic they looked as monstrous and distorted as the faces in an old film, *The Island of Doctor Moreau.* And then I looked again, but they were just average men and women, no more deeply involved than if this were a television play.

Dr. Graves gave me an encouraging nod, Ken's narrowed eyes smiled at me, making me feel almost as though he had taken my hand and was holding it in a warm clasp.

I was taken swiftly through the preliminary questions. I was Catherine Briggs, twenty-three, niece and only living relative of the late Mrs. Gerald Harcourt. I had come here expecting to attend her funeral.

The coroner—later I learned that he had been a friend of Aunt Geraldine's, or rather she had been his friend and had supported him when he wanted to be coroner—was gentle with me. He had an easy, relaxed voice, except when he lost his temper with young Smith, and he led me easily and quickly through my discovery of Tim Cooper's body.

"He was dead when you found him?"

"Oh, yes, he must have been. That is, I couldn't see his face. I was trying to get his foot free—it was caught somehow—and when I couldn't manage that, I tried to hold his head up so his face would be out of the water. And then Mr. Knight came and helped me, and then we knew he was dead."

"What happened then?"

From the beginning I had assumed that he would ask what seemed to me the inevitable question, whether I had ever seen the man before. I was so surprised that I blinked at him and he had to repeat his question.

"Oh, Mr. Knight said we must not move him and then he called the police."

"I'd like to know," Smith the irrepressible said, "how Miss Briggs happened to find the man."

The coroner started to speak, changed his mind. I was puzzled. I explained that the house was chilly and I had gone outside to walk in the sun where it was warmer.

The young man was determined. How did it happen that Mrs. Harcourt's heiress—if you were to believe the news, though he admitted you couldn't always—wasn't at the funeral?

Maine was glaring at the recalcitrant juror and, as he was both bigger and heavier, I hated to think of what was going to happen when we got out of this stuffy room.

I described the delays on the bus and then Captain Grieg got up to speak to the coroner, and sent a man out of the room. Then when the coroner told me to step down, Captain Grieg took my place to testify that the details of my trip had all been checked, that I had taken a bus which had been detoured and then had broken down and had to wait hours for a replacement. Then—he broke off as his man returned with a stoop-shouldered man with a thin face that was somehow familiar. Oh, of course, this was Bailey, the man at the bus station.

He looked around him without self-consciousness, nodded to a number of people, and took the seat that Captain Grieg had vacated for him. At the coroner's request he looked at me. Sure, that was Miss Briggs, the pretty one who looked so much like Mrs. Harcourt. Knew who she was the moment he clapped eyes

143

on her and told her so. She got off the twelve o'clock bus and left her suitcase at the bus station. Wanted to know how to get to the funeral and he'd told her she was too late and the only taxi that could take her was already at the church, maybe even at the cemetery by then. Told her how to get to the Old Mill, that she could walk it easy.

Whether it was because he was aware of an atmosphere of hostility and suspicion toward me or just general cussedness and an inclination to clown, Bailey went on to say he'd been surprised I brought only one suitcase. Most people seemed to expect to settle down forever at the Old Mill.

There was a little ripple of laughter; I could even detect a glimmer of amusement in the coroner's eyes, and then he dismissed Bailey in a hurry. The latter got up in his relaxed way, winked at me, and strolled out of the room on a wave of sympathetic laughter. I hoped someday to have an opportunity to thank him. He had changed the whole atmosphere of that room of self-appointed judges in regard to me. No one could believe now that I had killed Tim Cooper, and somehow that one suitcase had weighed heavily in my favor.

"Mr. Kendrick Knight," the coroner said, and Ken took the chair Bailey had vacated. The coroner politely asked his name, address, occupation.

"Will you describe what happened at the millstream, Mr. Knight, at the time when Miss Briggs found the body?"

"It was about twelve-thirty. I had just reached the Old Mill and I was going in when I saw Ca—Miss Briggs lying on the bank so close to the edge she nearly overbalanced. There was a man submerged and she was trying to hold his head out of water, in the hope

144

that he was alive. Of course, she was not strong enough to get him out. When I had turned him over and seen that he was dead, we went into the mill to call the police."

The coroner asked the question he had been so careful not to ask me. "Had you ever seen the man before?"

"Never."

"How did you happen to be there?" Smith asked.

"You," the goaded coroner exploded, "are not conducting this inquiry."

Smith was unabashed. "Well, someone should. A guy gets killed. A girl gets stabbed by what they tell us was a masked man. Maybe, according to rumor, Mrs. Harcourt was killed." He ignored the agitated sound of the coroner's hammer. His voice rose. "Is this a court of inquiry or isn't it? Here's a guy who is supposed to be one of Mrs. Harcourt's closest friends. Instead of going to her funeral, he's snooping around the mill just when someone gets killed there. I say the whole thing stinks."

"I think," Ken said coolly, "I had better answer these questions before there is any more confusion. I did not attend the funeral of Mrs. Harcourt because such—social observances—seemed meaningless to her. I came to the mill, expecting it to be unoccupied, because I wanted to look around. In my opinion Mrs. Harcourt was murdered and I wanted to find some proof, if there was any."

Even the irrepressible Mr. Smith was momentarily silenced. Then he asked, "Did you?"

"No, there was no opportunity to look around. Instead, I found another dead body."

"That's right. You're the one who found Mrs. Harcourt. How—"

"Mrs. Harcourt's death is not our concern at this time," the coroner said.

There was a disturbance in the back of the room and Leopold called out in his big, resonant voice, "I'd like to be heard, Mr. Coroner."

The coroner was shattered. The inquiry, which was to have been routine, had gotten completely out of control. Questions had been raised—awkward questions. The other deaths had been involved.

Leopold came forward, took the chair, gave his name as Leonard Winters, but said he preferred to use the name Leopold Wenski professionally. He was a pianist. There was a stir and a murmur of comment. This was the husband of the girl who had been stabbed the night before by a masked man.

What he had to say was said briefly, and it was completely devastating. Any hope the coroner had had of a routine inquiry went out of the window.

"Last night," he began, "my wife was murdered." As the coroner started to protest, he raised his voice. "I think she was murdered by the same person who killed the man they found in the millstream. I heard her say she intended to make her fortune. She was threatening someone. She knew who the killer was and she was issuing a warning. That's why the poor kid was stabbed."

"You are making totally irresponsible statements," the coroner told him.

"You mean I can't prove any of this," Leopold said calmly. "Yes, I know. That is up to the police. But the guy or gal who killed my wife is the one who brought her back from the cemetery. She left ahead of anyone else and there was time enough, when they got back, for this guy Cooper to have been killed. And I swear to

146

God I don't know who it was or I'd deal with this myself."

The situation was so completely out of hand that the coroner called for an adjournment.

II

"We're getting out of here," Ken said, forcing his way to my side.

"Cathy is going home with us," Maine told him.

"Like hell she is."

"What business is this of yours, Knight?"

"I intend to protect Cathy's interests."

The reporters and the silent crowd were listening avidly to this exchange. Then Arthur Mattheson laughed without humor. "A great many people seem eager to protect Miss Briggs's interests. Cathy, you'd be better off if I took you to Dr. Graves's house, as he suggested."

Ken waited, his hand warm on my arm. I hadn't said a word, but he seemed not to need any comment on my part. There was the barest trace of a smile on his lips. He pushed his way through the crowd and I flung up an arm to shield my face from the cameras. As luck would have it, he had parked some distance away and we had to make our way through that crowd of curious faces. When he had put me in the front seat, he got behind the wheel and shot away from the curb.

"Well," he said at length, "the fat's in the fire now."

"Things got out of hand, didn't they? Will that do much harm?"

"I'm not sure. Grieg's idea, of course, was to keep still about those attacks Cooper had made on you until he could get a line on who was paying him. He didn't want to put anyone on guard. But on the whole it's better to get things out in the open. At least now they're going to have to produce alibis for every single one of them. Good for Leopold. I wouldn't have believed he had it in him. By the way, what happened to Nell? She's the last person to have missed that business this morning, I would have thought."

"She was hysterical and Dr. Graves put her under sedation."

"Why?"

"Last night she walked the floor for hours, and she was afraid to take the sleeping pills Dr. Graves left. No matter what Leopold says, she wasn't faking this morning. She was scared out of her wits. When Dr. Graves gave her that shot and she knew she'd be sleeping, she was terrified, just terrified."

"What do you think it's all about, Cathy?"

"Nell, you mean? I'm not sure. She seems to be involved in this whole ugly mess in some way."

"You mean that she is afraid of being found out?"

"All I'm sure of is that she is afraid."

Ken turned in the seat to smile at me. "Come on, Cathy, give! By the way, any place in particular where you'd like to go? Any errands to do?"

"I don't want to go back to the mill; at least, not right away."

"But you are going back?"

"I'm going to stick to the terms of the will if it kills me."

"As it might well do. No, don't look like that. You're going to be watched day and night. Well, the carriage awaits. Where to, lady?"

"I need some clothes, sweaters and a warm skirt, things like that. Only I haven't enough money."

"I have one of those credit cards that's supposed to be all things to all men. Let's see how it works. We'll have to go to Bennington if you want clothes. All right?"

"All right." I slumped in the seat, resting my tight neck against the back. For the first time that morning I relaxed. But not for long.

"I'm still waiting to hear about Nell," Ken reminded me, and I remembered that this was not a normal shopping tour.

So I said that Leopold thought Nell was the only one who had fought with his wife. Sonia had been jealous. And Nell had referred to him as a servant, as though she'd stoop so low. And Leopold had said—well, anyone—my voice trailed off.

"Including me?" Ken's voice was without expression.

"Including you, I suppose. And Nell said I had you and Maine but to keep my hands off Arthur, and she began to scream."

Ken looked at me uneasily. "Look here, Cathy—"

"I don't want to hear about it." I hadn't meant to sound so angry. Perhaps Nell couldn't help being what she was. If Ken had been among the men in her life, it didn't mean a thing. At least not to me. But the depths of my resentment, my rebellion at the idea, brought home to me how I felt about Ken.

My voice, I suppose, had been a dead giveaway. There was the faintest trace of a smile on Ken's lips. "All right. Keep your shirt on, lady. Tell me the rest."

"Nell has a necklace that belonged to Aunt Geraldine. Maine found it in her room and demanded to know how she got it. She said she'd found it at the motel after Aunt Geraldine left and brought it home for safekeeping. Something like that."

"Go on."

"When we searched each other, she said I'd better marry Maine, that it would be my only chance."

"You mean she was threatening you?"

"Or warning me. I honestly don't know which."

"Well, well. By the way, what did Grieg have to say to you as I was hauling you out of there?"

"He said not to leave town. There would be an inquest on Sonia next Monday, and I'd have to stay for that as well as for the postponed inquest on Cooper."

"What was this whole deal about a whirlwind courtship? I heard that you were engaged to Maine, then you denied it, saying he was trying to protect you. What was it all about?"

I told him about Maine's proposal. It wasn't altogether or even primarily because of the Harcourt money. I honestly believed he was worried about my safety. When Ken made a derisive sound, I described that queer and frightening moment when I had thought Guthrie was going to push me into the millstream and Maine had shouted and run toward him, his face dead white, and the shocked look in Guthrie's face. It was after that Maine had asked me to marry him.

"Guthrie!" Ken exclaimed. "He's about the only one I haven't really suspected at one time or another. He doesn't act on things, he runs away from them."

"That's what Leopold said, but—"

"Are you sure you didn't imagine it?"

"I'm not sure he meant me to drown. But I was afraid. The millstream is very deep at that point. It's the spot where—"

When I did not go on, Ken said flatly. "That's where Grace died. I suppose Harcourt told you that. You'll have to know, of course, as things are." When I made no comment, he said slowly, "As things are between

150

us. Between you and me. And don't ask me what I mean."

He went on quietly. Grace had been defenseless, sweet, timid, lacking in self-confidence and in trust. The impression that came to me, without words, was of a man touched by that gentle creature and marrying her with more tenderness and compassion than love. He had brought her to Milltown and bought the local weekly and she was much happier than she had been in New York. More at ease.

And then she had met Arthur Mattheson. Ken's voice changed. It was like a cold wind in the car. The impact of the man's personality and his charm had been devastating. Grace had fallen headlong in love with him, but her infatuation had brought no happiness. She felt guilty about Ken because she believed that he had sacrificed his future for her sake, but her need for Arthur was more than she could bear. At length he persuaded her to divorce Ken and marry him.

"Poor Grace! She couldn't face me and tell me her decision." There was compassion mingled with deep anger in Ken's voice. "She left me a note and then— well, I suppose she couldn't bring herself to leave me and she couldn't give up Mattheson. So she chose the only other way out and she threw herself into the mill-stream."

After a long time Ken said, "This is the past, Cathy. We'll have to keep it there. No good ever comes of looking back over our shoulders. The world's ahead."

He slowed down to drive into the lovely town of Bennington, with its beautiful church and its enchanting Revolutionary houses.

"Let's forget it for now, shall we, Cathy? Just try for a little while to enjoy yourself."

And so help me, I did. We had lunch at the Paradise, with frosty cocktails that warmed as they went down, and marvelous food and we laughed a lot. Ken was easy to talk to. He was, as I had supposed, a big city man with a lot of varied experience; he had known amusing people and he had interesting sidelights on them. I like the way his mind worked, and the flashes of laughter that lit up his talk. In fact, I liked Ken.

It would, in fact, have been a completely happy afternoon if it hadn't been for what happened at the very last.

Ken's credit card seemed to work, and later I bought a deep red wool skirt and a bulky white sweater; a blue wool dress that fitted as though it had been made on me, and a soft, misty, purplish gray silk.

No one in the store seemed to recognize me. The clerks apparently assumed that Ken and I were man and wife, and it was easier not to undeceive them.

Ken signed the bill and while I waited for the packages, he left me to buy a tobacco pouch and get some different brand of tobacco for his pipe.

I had moved away from the counter and I was walking around a circular rack and momentarily out of sight, when I heard the talk.

"Gosh," the cashier whispered to the clerk who had waited on me and who had seemed so blandly ignorant of my identity, "they must be bride and groom. He doesn't mind spending money on her."

"He can afford it," the clerk said. "Not just because she's coming into millions—that's the Briggs girl who's mixed up in the Old Mill murders—but because he inherited a wad when his first wife died up there. I didn't realize who he was until I saw his name on the credit card. That's Kendrick Knight."

13

Several times on the drive back from Bennington, Ken started to speak to me and changed his mind. He was aware that something had happened to destroy the lighthearted mood that had arisen out of the lunch and the shopping expedition. There was a growing picture in my mind and it seemed to me that I had to abolish it before it took final shape, before it became complete and irrevocable.

"Ken," I said impulsively before I was too afraid to ask, "how did you happen to find Aunt Geraldine's body at a time when everyone was supposed to be away from the mill?"

"She asked me to go." When I made no comment, he added, "She sent me a note and asked whether I'd check on the place. The work was supposed to be done, but she did not want to return until the house was thoroughly warm. It's big you know, with a lot of space; that open staircase makes it hard as hell to heat adequately. So I drove out and found her."

After a while I asked, "Did you keep her note?"

There was no trace of a smile on Ken's lips now. "I didn't keep the note," he said evenly. "You can read it two ways, Cathy. Either there was no note and I lured her out to the mill to kill her or there was a note and someone wanted me to find her." As he pulled up at the curb, I asked, "Where are we?"

It was one of the big white Colonial houses on Main Street, with a lot of land, and the outbuildings all attached the way they are in Maine, so you can go from the main house to the barns without being out of doors.

"My house. The office and printing plant are in the back. Do you mind if I stop to pick up my mail before I take you home?"

"Of course not."

"I'll just be a minute. Or—won't you come in?"

A horn sounded and Arthur drove up behind Ken's car. He came around to me. His eyes took in the packages on the back seat, and I think he must have sensed the tension between us.

"I'm going out to the mill," he said. "Want a lift?"

"Why, thanks." I opened the door and almost tumbled out. "It will save Ken the trip. Those packages—"

While Arthur removed the packages, I thanked Ken rather breathlessly, but I avoided looking at him. He made no comment at all. He did not look at me, but he watched Arthur. I wouldn't have wanted anyone to look at me like that.

When Arthur had settled me in the seat beside him, my packages on the back seat, he gave me a long grave look. "God, was I glad to see you drive up! I was beginning to worry—"

"You've been waiting for me?" I was surprised.

"I had a talk with Captain Grieg. There's not much of an organization to call on, you know, though he is getting men from other communities, as many as they can spare, but he has no one to ride herd on you. So I offered to take on the job."

"But why should it be necessary?"

154

"There's a lot of money at stake, Cathy. After that monkey wrench got thrown into the inquest this morning, the police are marshaling all the men they can get to check alibis, backgrounds, all that. They'll turn up every record that exists on everyone in the case, and you'd be surprised how many records there are, even of the most obscure people. They are efficient, and what's to be dug up, they will find. Depend on that. But—it takes time, not simply to establish the facts but to determine how much they mean."

"You're talking about the Harcourts, the ones who lose if I inherit?"

"It isn't limited to the Harcourts," Arthur said. "By the way, I take it that Maine's attempt to convince people that you are engaged to him was just so much hot air."

"He thought it would be best." After a moment I added, "So did Nell." Arthur made no comment about Nell. "You say it isn't limited to the Harcourts. But who else—?"

"Well," Arthur said, "the first thing the police turned up was the fact that Leonard Winters' fingerprints are on record. Breaking and entering. He was only fourteen at the time, so he wasn't sentenced. Stole a television set and sold it for money to continue his music lessons. He'd do a lot for his music."

"But he wouldn't have killed Sonia. Never."

Arthur gave me his warm smile. "So sure of that?" he said teasingly.

I nodded emphatically. "Who introduced him to Aunt Geraldine in the first place?"

"I haven't the slightest idea. I never heard her mention it."

"How long have the Wenskis been at the mill?"

"Not long. Six weeks or two months. No more than that. I remember trying to dissuade Mrs. Harcourt when she told me about her plans. I said that she would be wiser to provide him with a room somewhere and help him financially if she wanted to, but it was risky to take a stranger into her own house like that. Actually it turned out to be two strangers, because he married Sonia and brought her along with him. But Mrs. Harcourt wouldn't listen to me. It's the only time she ever refused to take my advice." After a long pause, Arthur said somberly, "Except the last time, except when she drew that second will without telling me."

"Do you think it was very unjust?"

He stretched out a hand and covered both of mine, which were clasped on my lap. "It isn't the disposition of the estate that bothers me. Actually, I think she was quite justified. The property will be in better hands with you in charge. It was only—well, I suppose the truth is that my vanity was hurt because she took so drastic a step without consulting me. Of course, Knight must have suggested the idea."

"You dislike Ken very much, don't you?" I said bluntly.

He nodded, his eyes on the road. "I hate his guts," he told me succinctly. "One thing I am looking forward to, when the police really start digging, is having them strip that plausible guy, inch by inch, of his pretensions."

"What do you think they would find?"

"God knows. He's so damnably plausible. He could wrap a woman as intelligent as Mrs. Harcourt around his finger without half trying. He could persuade an exquisite creature like Grace to marry him. There have

156

been a few moments when I've wondered—I've been afraid—he was making an impression on you."

"Afraid?" It wasn't a very good effort, but it was the best I could do.

And then, for the second time that day, a man was telling me about Grace Knight. She had been one of those poor little rich girls, poor because she had a slight limp from polio and she had been emotionally scarred by it. Knight's ability to charm her and win her confidence wasn't, after all, so strange. He was a superb psychologist. And he had taken her away from her family and friends, settled her in Milltown where she was completely dependent on him for friendship, amusement, society, whatever.

"I met her," Arthur told me, "at a small dinner party Dr. Graves gave. She was not only his patient, but he was very fond of her. No one could help being fond of her. She was an exquisite creature, Cathy. She lit up as though there were candles behind her eyes when you made her laugh. She—"

When he went on, his voice was steady. "She was the loveliest thing I had ever seen and the sweetest and the most vulnerable. You longed to protect her. She was lonely and I was lonely. What happened, of course, is that I fell in love with her and she with me. I wanted to go straight to Knight and tell him the truth— she was so incapable of fighting her own battles!" His hand clenched, beat lightly on the wheel. "But she said that she must do this thing herself. She was going to tell him that we loved each other and that she was going to Reno to get a divorce. She—I let her face him alone. Oh, God, Cathy! I'll never forgive myself. I let her face him alone. So they found her late that evening in the millstream."

I was beginning to shake and I sat fighting down waves of nausea. I wanted him to stop, but I didn't dare speak, didn't dare open my clenched jaws.

"Dr. Graves said she had had a heart attack. Until the size of the estate she had left Knight became known—most people around here had thought she was an obscure little thing—her death was regarded as a tragic accident. After that, a kind of garbled rumor got out, started by Knight himself, that it was suicide while of unsound mind. But, as sure as I live and breathe, Kendrick Knight put his wife in that mill-stream, Cathy."

I was incapable of speaking. Arthur looked at his watch. "Four-thirty. Let's go somewhere and have a drink before I take you back to the mill. I could use one."

As it happened, he chose the place to which Ken Knight had taken me. At this hour the dining room was empty, the lights had not been turned on. The swinging doors to the kitchen had been propped open and voices were coming from there. The bar was empty except for the bartender, who was slicing oranges and preparing lemon peel for cocktails.

When our drinks were before us, the bartender said, "If you want anything, just sing out. I've got to get some stuff from the kitchen."

"Go ahead," Arthur told him.

Seeing his face, even in the dim light of the bar, I was aware of the ravages caused by that emotional outbreak. Of all the men I had encountered since I reached Milltown, he was the one least likely, I would have thought, to surrender to any emotional display. He caught my eyes fixed on his face and smiled, the warm attractive smile that was so large a part of his charm.

"Poor Cathy," he said gently. "I wonder why I had to burden you with all that! No, actually, I know quite well why it was. Try to forget that story. It was all over two years ago. It was in another country and, besides," for a moment his mouth twisted, "the wench is dead."

He raised his glass. "To happier times."

It took all my control to raise my own glass without spilling it. I smiled back. "To happier times."

"That's my girl! Are you, Cathy? I thought I would never fall in love again, but it doesn't seem to be anything man can control. Will you add to your conquests a struggling young lawyer?" When I made no reply, he said, "At least, you can put me on the list."

I laughed. "I'll do that."

At something in my expression his face lightened. He reached for my hand. "You're cold!"

"Just nerves. Too much has happened. I haven't been able to absorb it all."

"You will," he said confidently. "Another drink?"

I shook my head and he called the bartender, who came back with a basket of fruit and, to my surprise, a bowl of eggs.

It seemed that our trip back to the mill was to be made in unbroken silence. I almost hoped it would be. Then Arthur asked what Aunt Geraldine had told me about the Harcourts. Not much, I admitted. Apparently they had resented the way the Harcourt money had been diverted from them, though most of it had been earned by Gerald, who had a right to dispose of it as he liked.

Of course, Arthur said absently, as though he were really thinking of something else, it must have been maddening to see it practically in reach and then have it swept away again. Nell had been twice divorced and she had no alimony; she had never done any work except for a few months, between husbands, when she had apparently been a Go Go girl in some nightclub in Phoenix. Evidently she had written to my aunt, saying that she was desperately hard up, and she had been invited to come for a visit.

"And that," Arthur said dryly, "was the opening wedge, the foot inside the door. She settled down with no intention of leaving. Then Guthrie took a chance on coming back to this country, and he moved in. Maine was the last to come. He didn't want to, to the best of my belief. He's a weak sister in many ways but independent as a hog on ice. He writes highbrow articles and short stories without plots for minor magazines. Now and then he has a job doing television scripts, but he hasn't seemed to be interested in money, which makes him a maverick in that family."

"Then why does he stay on at the Old Mill?"

"Nell," Arthur said succinctly. "Over and over, she gets out of the frying pan into the fire. Patient Maine is always there to haul her out again. But someday, of course, she'll get into so much trouble that no one can help her."

"I think," I told him, "she's in trouble now. She's frightened, Arthur. She's terribly frightened."

II

Maine's MG was in the driveway, and so was the Cadillac. When Arthur had shut off the motor, he turned toward me with an air of decision. I had to forestall him in some way.

"What's that?"

He listened and then shook his head in mock disbe-

160

lief. "The ruling passion," he murmured in amusement.

Apparently the studio had had the seals removed. Leopold was playing the piano, doing that ornate, technically impossible transcription of "Pictures at an Exhibition." Apparently he was, like Horowitz and Gilels, preparing to be the kind of musician who has them lying in the aisles at the end of a concert.

"It is a ruling passion," I said half defensively. "There aren't many people—how many? perhaps a dozen—who can play like that, and he's only at the beginning."

"Even with his wife just dead."

"Even with his wife just dead," I agreed. "I suppose a really great artist has to be selfish, completely self-centered. Like a great criminal."

Arthur put back his head and shouted with laughter, the first genuine laugh I had heard in days. "Cathy, you are wonderful." He picked up my hand, kissed the palm lightly, closed my fingers over it, and put my hand back on the car seat.

While he collected my packages, I went to the door and rang the bell. In a moment Maine came to open it, and his tired face lighted in relief when he saw me.

"Thank God, Cathy! I was beginning to worry."

That was what Arthur had said. "But why?"

He laid a hand on my shoulder while we walked into the living room. "You can ask that—with what has been happening here? Nothing seems safe or right or normal."

I laughed. "Except Leopold practicing."

"If you can call anything about Leopold normal." Maine turned his head quickly and I saw his father coming from the dining room. There was a nervous tic that made him blink constantly, and I knew that this wasn't his first drink of the day.

Arthur came in behind us, his arms filled with the packages. "Where do you want these, Cathy?"

"Put them anywhere. I'll take them up to my room later."

"Why not let me do it for you? Where have they put you?"

"I have Aunt Geraldine's room, the one on the west side. But there's no hurry."

He hesitated and then put the boxes down on one of the couches. Seeing Maine's surprised look, I described my shopping expedition to Bennington with Ken Knight. If I were to stay on any longer in Vermont, I'd simply have to have more clothes, and the temperature here was much colder than in my part of Pennsylvania.

"I wondered how you had happened to change escorts, as you might say, in midstream."

"Suppose," Guthrie suggested, "we all have a little bracer."

Maine and Arthur spoke at almost the same moment. "It's early for a drink."

"It's never too early." Guthrie surveyed Arthur. "And if I'm not mistaken, you've already had a drink. So—"

"I'll call Nell to join us," Maine said. "Suppose we wait for her. Then we'll have to go out for dinner. Leopold says he can't do much but open cans and boil potatoes and fry bacon and eggs. We all need a decent meal."

"Can't Nell—" Arthur began.

Maine shrugged. "Nell won't," he said succinctly. "She says if she's not the mistress here, she'll take no responsibility."

"I can cook," I offered. "I'll see what there is. There should be plenty of cold turkey left to slice and I can make some scalloped potatoes and heat up the creamed onions. We barely touched them. And there is another pumpkin pie."

Maine slid his arm around my shoulders before I was aware of what he was doing. "I'm getting myself a little cook," he said, and kissed my cheek.

At the expression on Arthur's face I said hastily, "I'll take up these packages and freshen up."

"I'll call Nell," Maine said.

"Is she still asleep? It will take almost an hour for the potatoes, so there's no hurry."

"I don't know what Dr. Graves gave her when she went to pieces that way this morning, but she has slept all day long. Time she was awake." In spite of his attempt to speak quietly, there was uneasiness in Maine's voice.

Guthrie stood watching us, his eyelids twitching with that nervous tic. He turned quietly and made his way out to the dining room and the bar.

Without a word Arthur took the packages out of my arms and I followed him up the stairs, while Maine watched us, a queer trapped look on his face.

Arthur put the packages down on a chair and took a quick look at the room. "Very nice. Mrs. Harcourt managed to make a room a frame for her, didn't she?"

I understood what he meant. "But it's the wrong frame for me."

He smiled. "It's your frame, too. You're incredibly like her, you know." He came to touch my cheek lightly with a fingertip. "It's too soon to tell you how beautiful you are. But later—"

He went out swiftly. I heard him knock on Nell's door. Then he knocked louder.

"Nell! Nearly six o'clock. How about joining us for a drink? Cathy's going to be cook tonight."

I had closed the bathroom door. When I had washed, brushed my hair, and repaired my make-up, I came back into the bedroom. Arthur was pounding on Nell's door.

"Nell!" he shouted. "Are you all right?"

When I flung open the door of my room, the trooper who had been left in charge and who had, apparently, been taking a turn around the grounds, came running up the stairs, passing Maine. Guthrie stood at the foot, staring upward.

"Have any of you seen Nell today?" Arthur demanded. When he saw their expressions he did not wait for the trooper. He moved back and then ran at the door, striking it with his shoulder. The flimsy lock snapped and he catapulted into the room.

14

Arthur came out of Nell's bedroom and closed the door gently. There was no color in his face. He had a letter in his hand which he gave to Maine without a word.

"Dead?" Maine asked, his voice sounding oddly flat.

Arthur nodded and wiped his face.

Maine said, "You're sure?" As he started to open the door, Arthur held out a hand.

"Better not. Yes, I'm sure." He drew the unresisting Maine away from the door.

"Was it an accident?"

"It can't have been. Poison of some sort, I'd say."

"Who could have done that to Nell?"

"She did it herself, Maine. The door was locked."

The trooper pushed past the two men and opened the door of Nell's room. Three or four minutes must have gone by before he came out and closed the door. Because of the broken lock, he couldn't fasten it.

"Go downstairs, please. All of you. I must call in."

There were, as I have said, three telephone extensions: one in the living room behind the fireplace, a second in the kitchen, the third on a table in the upstairs hallway. It was this telephone the trooper used while Maine stood leaning against the wall as though he could not move; I waited, frozen, in the doorway of my bedroom; and Arthur wiped his face with a handkerchief. Downstairs, Guthrie had turned blindly and headed back for his usual panacea in the dining room.

In the quiet house there was no sound but the pyrotechnics coming from the studio. It was the first time I had been angry with Leopold, but now I kept saying silently, "Stop it! Stop it!" though I knew the music could not disturb Nell.

Then the trooper was speaking quietly. There had been another death at the Old Mill . . . Mrs. Glenn . . . Poison, apparently. . . . Impossible to say. No one had seen her all day. . . . Of course he had been on duty. No one had entered the room, which was locked on the inside. . . . She'd been given some shot by Dr. Graves that morning. . . . No one but her father and brother and the guy at the piano. . . . Mattheson and Miss Briggs had just come in. . . . Broke open the door when Mrs. Glenn did not answer.

Arthur touched Maine's arm, realized how dazed he was, and led him downstairs. I followed them. When he saw Guthrie, Arthur gave an irritable exclamation and took away the drink the older man had just poured for himself.

"You've had all you can handle, Harcourt. You've got to pull yourself together. Nell's dead. Do you understand? She killed herself. The police are on their way and you must be ready to answer questions." He shook Guthrie's shoulder. "Are you paying attention?"

The tic was accentuated. Guthrie blinked at him. "Shertainly," he said with dignity, and collapsed into a chair.

"God! That's more than I can take," Arthur said, with the first break in his control, and he went along the passage and flung open the studio door. "Stop that," he shouted.

The music broke off. "I've got to practice."

"Not now you haven't."

"Why not?"

"Mrs. Glenn has committed suicide. The police are on their way."

There was a jangled sound and then Leopold exclaimed, "I don't believe it!"

When Arthur returned, looking rather ashamed of his outburst, he glanced at Guthrie, who had subsided in his chair and was staring blankly ahead of him; then at Maine, whose face was empty of all expression, all feeling. He went into the dining room and poured a drink, forced the glass into Maine's hand. "You need this."

Maine sipped obediently and finally set down the empty glass. There was a little color in his face now.

"Better?"

There was a faint smile on Maine's lips. "Better? With Nell dead? Why in heaven's name did she do it, Arthur? She—I've never known anyone who enjoyed life so much, who had such a—such an appetite for living. I've always thought she was the kind of person who would rather be alive even if she were deaf and blind and dumb and crippled and in constant pain."

"Didn't she make any explanation?"

"Explanation? I told you I haven't seen her since this morning when Dr. Graves gave her that shot to quiet her."

"I mean in her note."

"What note?"

"The note I found in her room. I gave it to you. For God's sake, get on the beam, Maine!"

Maine groped in his pockets and pulled out a sealed envelope. Typed on it was the word "Maine."

There was a scream of sirens as the police heralded

their approach. The unhappy trooper went to the door to admit them. Captain Grieg had nothing fatherly about him now. His face was hard and grim. "Where is she?"

"Upstairs. Her room."

"Stay where you are, all of you. Where's that fellow Wenski?"

"In the studio."

"Get him," Grieg told one of the troopers. "Get him in here. And no talking."

He went up the stairs, followed by what seemed like a whole army of police, and I heard a sharp exchange outside Nell's room.

"No, sir. No one entered this room after I came on duty. The lady was brought up by Dr. Graves and me. She was half asleep at the time. She locked her door. I never heard a sound out of her after that. Nothing happened until Mr. Mattheson got here and tried to awaken her."

The door opened and closed. Men were walking in Nell's room. The footsteps stopped abruptly at the entrance to her bathroom. Then there were low comments, activity of some sort. I didn't try to hear. I didn't want to hear.

Downstairs, under the watchful eye of a trooper, we didn't speak at all. Once I saw Leopold staring at Maine in a puzzled sort of way; once Arthur met my gaze across the room and smiled his warm encouraging smile.

It had long been dark, the early darkness of late autumn, when car lights appeared and Arthur started to go to the door. The trooper watching us said abruptly, "I'll do that." He opened the door. "Oh, glad to see you, Doctor. You're to go right up."

"Who is it?" Dr. Graves asked.

"Mrs. Glenn. In her room, Doctor."

"Nell? Dead? Good God! I thought it was Nell who—"

"You thought she killed them?" Leopold asked. "Yes, so did I. There were—reasons, and Sonia would have made trouble for her."

Dr. Graves turned to Maine. "I'm sorry, but perhaps this is best. She was in this mess, Maine, right up to her ears. I've traced the mental institution with which she got in touch, trying to sound them out on mental incompetence. She wanted Mrs. Harcourt committed. I suppose we can say unsound mind. So much violence. So much cold-bloodedness. Yes, we can say unsound mind."

"No," Maine said, "I can't make myself believe she was a killer. She stole the pearls probably. She took the clothes. She was—greedy. But she wouldn't have hurt Sonia. Her interests weren't that lasting or that deep. She didn't want to—keep them."

"Leopold," I asked, "who introduced you to my aunt?"

"Sonia." He spoke dully. "Someone said she'd be likely to help me."

"And who told Sonia?"

"I don't know."

Dr. Graves looked old and drawn and anxious. He came to touch my shoulder with a gentle hand. "I'm going to insist on taking you home with me, my dear. This has become a pesthouse. A nightmare."

"Thank you. If they'll let me go."

"They'll let you go," he said grimly. He picked up his bag and went upstairs, his feet heavy and tired on the metal treads.

It was after seven when the men trooped down the stairs and herded us into the dining room. For a moment I thought Arthur was going to protest and then, as Grieg made a slight gesture, he got promptly to his feet and led the way. I knew then that they were going to bring Nell down and take her away.

After a while Dr. Graves came to tell me, "Grieg says you can come to my house tonight. My housekeeper will prepare a room for you. I'd like to take you with me now, but they have some questions to ask. When did you eat last?"

"I had lunch in Bennington."

"Nothing since?"

"No."

"How about the rest of you?"

"We've been sitting here under the eyes of Hawkshaw the detective," Arthur said tartly, with a glance at the trooper. "There's been no chance to eat."

"Well, you'll have to have something."

"We aren't hungry," Maine said.

"Speak for yourself," the doctor told him. "You may have no appetite, but you are all bound to be hungry. I'll arrange with Grieg." There was a mutter of conversation in the living room and Grieg came out.

"Okay, you're to have something to eat. Can you cook?" he asked Leopold.

"I can," I said.

"Go ahead then. I'll leave a trooper with you."

"What do you think will happen to her in her own house?" Maine demanded.

"Judging by four bodies in a few days, I'd say almost anything could happen."

So I sliced the cold turkey and prepared parsley

potatoes, found an aspic salad that Sonia had made, and cut the second pumpkin pie.

Maine set the table and helped me serve the scratch meal. At my suggestion, the trooper joined us. We didn't talk. Whether or not it was the presence of the police, none of us had anything to say.

With Maine's help I cleared the table and turned on the dishwasher. Then we waited. It must have been nine-thirty when Grieg came back to the mill. He looked desperately tired, but there was more than that in his face.

"A few days ago," he began abruptly, taking an uncomfortable straight chair as though afraid he would succumb to exhaustion in a more comfortable one, "I'd have laughed at the idea of a house being jinxed. But there have been four violent deaths on these premises within a matter of days: Mrs. Harcourt, Tim Cooper, Sonia Wenski, and now Nell Glenn."

"But Nell—" Maine began.

Grieg's expression was rather embarrassed as he looked at Maine. "I guess that Mrs. Glenn's death isn't the worst thing that could happen. It wraps up the case."

Arthur expelled a long breath. "You mean it was Nell Glenn who was responsible for those deaths?"

"We found the kind of evidence we need in her room: Tim Cooper's billfold, for one thing. Some letters addressed to Miss Briggs and written by Mrs. Harcourt. The ones she lost."

Guthrie straightened up. "Nell?" His eyes blinked like mad. "Not Nell! She promised she was going to make a place for the old man when she inherited the mill."

Arthur clutched at Guthrie's shoulder and his hand tightened.

"What you are saying," Maine spoke slowly, still sounding as though he were in a state of shock, "is that Nell killed three people and then killed herself. Nell! Suicide? Never. Anyhow, how could she—"

Dr. Graves had done a swift preliminary investigation, Grieg told him. Nell Glenn had been found lying on the floor in her bathroom. She had started to clean her teeth. There was cyanide in the toothpaste.

"No one would ever do it that way!" I exclaimed. "No one in his right mind."

"You'd be surprised," Grieg commented.

"But, Maine, didn't she explain in that letter?"

"What letter?"

"The one Arthur found in her room and gave you."

Maine, acting like a sleepwalker, searched his pockets and drew out the still sealed letter. After a momentary hesitation he surrendered it to the captain.

The latter held it carefully by the edge. "Did Mrs. Glenn know how to type?"

"Yes, she studied typing after her first divorce. She thought she might get an office job."

"Is there a typewriter in the house?"

"Of course. Mine. In my room."

Captain Grieg picked up a letter opener from the table, slit the envelope, drew out the single sheet of paper. No one moved as he read it slowly. No one seemed to breathe while we waited.

"So," he said at last. He read it aloud:

"By now I suppose the captain knows why I killed them. If he hasn't found out, Leopold will tell him. I can't stand waiting any longer, and this way is the easiest one out. At least it's quick. I can't say I'm really sorry, except that it didn't work. On five million dollars the world would have been mine. But Cooper threatened and Sonia knew. Sooner or later she'd have

172

put the bite on. Marry Cathy if you can. *Sauve qui peut*. Be seeing you in the Elysian Fields. Nell."

There was a long silence in the room. Then Leopold, aware of the eyes fixed on his face, said, "There's nothing I could tell you, Captain, that I haven't told. Sonia didn't confide in me because she was up to something she thought I wouldn't like. We weren't married long, but I knew that much about her."

"You have a record, haven't you?"

Leopold dropped his air of defiance. There was something of defeat, of hopelessness, in the swift gesture of his hands, almost a kind of surrender. "When you took the fingerprints, I was afraid of that. Look, I was only fourteen. My teacher said she couldn't afford to give me another lesson unless I paid. My mother was dead and my father thought music was for sissies. I had to play! I had to! But if that comes out, no matter how good I am, it will finish me. Please, Captain, please!"

Grieg stopped him. "It depends. You know I can't promise until I know all the facts. Now then," and he glanced at one of the troopers who opened a notebook, "let's see where you all were today."

"But no one got into Nell's room," Maine protested. "The trooper on guard said so. Anyhow, it was suicide. It—" His voice trailed off. There was the queerest look on his face, half horror, half hope. "No, that's impossible. The letter is a fake."

"She must have written the letter," Arthur pointed out. "The room was guarded all day long."

"You think someone killed my girl?" Guthrie demanded thickly.

"Yes, I do." Maine's voice had risen, was high and excited. "Don't you remember, Dad? Nell didn't know a single word of French."

173

15

Maine's bombshell exploded the theory that Nell's death had solved the case. It had simply added another victim. We were all to get out of the mill for the night, by police order, apparently on the theory that the whole house might be booby-trapped. The Harcourts and Leopold were to go to a motel under guard. Arthur was permitted to go home. I was to be allowed to stay at Dr. Graves's house.

It was while I was packing my bag to go to the doctor's that I had an unexpected interview with Maine. Arthur had gone, gone reluctantly and only after trying to persuade Captain Grieg to let him drive me to Dr. Graves.

"We'll keep an eye on her," Grieg said. "She'll be all right."

"You kept an eye on Mrs. Glenn. No one could have got into her room," Arthur reminded him somberly, "but she died."

"Miss Briggs," Grieg warned me, "don't take any of your cosmetics with you. Nothing at all? Understand? No toothpaste or mouthwash, no cold cream or lipstick. We can get what you need from the drugstore."

"The drugstore will be closed by now," Arthur reminded him.

"Then she can wait until morning to clean her teeth,

can't she? I'll have some stuff picked up for her," the captain promised.

Arthur put a supporting arm around me and must have been aware of my stiff resistance. "You'll be all right. Ask Dr. Graves for something to help you sleep."

"No!" I cried in a panic, and was reminded of Nell crying out in the same fear of becoming unconscious and helpless.

"Look here." Arthur sounded startled. "Look here, Captain. Is it possible—that is, could Dr. Graves conceivably have made a mistake in the amount of dope he gave Mrs. Glenn this morning?"

"Graves!"

"Well, it begins to strike me as odd, you know. We've been casting suspicions all over the place. But how about our good doctor? Knight's wife leaves him money and she dies. Mrs. Harcourt leaves him money and she dies. He gives Mrs. Glenn a shot that's supposed to act as a sedative and she dies. He's right on tap all the time, isn't he? He could easily have got at Maine's typewriter. If Mrs. Glenn knew something—"

"Are you trying to set Graves up as the killer?"

"I'm simply making a few simple points."

"And what do you hope to achieve by that?"

"Just this." Arthur was coldly angry and he was also, I thought, dangerous. "If anything happens to Catherine Briggs because she spends a night in his house, I'm going to pull it down on him, brick by brick. And, so help me God, I'll pull down the whole police force before I am through."

Grieg hesitated, impressed in spite of himself by Arthur's cold rage. "What would you prefer to do, Miss Briggs? Mr. Mattheson is right about your safety being at stake. Have you any preference? Please understand that we will do our best to protect you, but—Mrs. Glenn was apparently being protected and we couldn't save her."

"I think I'd like to go to Dr. Graves."

"You trust him that much?" Arthur asked.

"Trust is sort of at a premium right now, isn't it? But there was something—I think he loved Aunt Geraldine and I don't believe he would ever hurt me. I don't believe he hurt her. He couldn't. He loved her. It isn't a matter of reason, just of faith, I guess."

"You're taking the chance," Grieg said. "I don't feel that I should influence you."

But in the long run it was agreed that I would go to Dr. Graves.

"I'll call you in the morning," Arthur said. He went out and I heard him drive away.

Guthrie was blundering around in his room when I went upstairs. He stumbled and fell against a table so that a lamp crashed on the floor. A trooper went hurrying into his room.

Maine took advantage of that moment to step inside the door of my room and then his arms were around me, he was holding me against him. I could feel him shaking. "Oh, Cathy! Oh, Cathy!"

I released myself more gently than I had intended to. "I'm terribly sorry about Nell."

"In a way I'm almost glad."

"Glad!"

"It's been hell. Absolute hell. My sister or my father. I thought one of them was the killer for that damned Harcourt money. You can't imagine what it's been like. But now I know it wasn't Nell and it wasn't Dad. He would never have hurt Nell. She was the only person he was ever fond of. So in a way I'm almost glad."

"But it narrows the number of suspects, doesn't it?"

The trooper had come back and was standing in the doorway. Maine paid no attention to him. "You're so young and impressionable. I wish to God you'd marry me. I'm really in love with you; I was at first sight. And I'm a patient man, Cathy. I could wait. And you would be safe. That way you would be safe."

Something in his face warned me. "You know who killed them!"

"I think so. This time I must be right. Cathy, for God's sake don't trust anyone. Not now."

"On your way, bud," the trooper said, not unkindly. Maine bent, kissed me quickly, and went to his own room to pack.

"Ready, miss?" The trooper picked up my suitcase and followed me down the lovely dramatic staircase, through the living room, and out to the waiting police car.

II

Dr. Graves's house was spacious and dignified, the furniture was beautiful, and waxed like a mirror. The whole house smelled of beeswax and potpourri. His housekeeper was tall and gaunt, a thin-lipped woman who knew most of the village gossip and a great deal about the doctor's patients, as his office was connected with the house, but repeated nothing of what she knew.

She looked about as homey and sentimental as a broomstick but, late as it was—after eleven when we reached the house—she was neatly dressed and her hair pulled back in a bun.

"Come in, you poor thing." She half carried me up the stairs to a big guest room, where the covers had been turned back. The linen sheets were scented with lavender.

She began to undress me, pulled my nightgown over my head, all without exchanging a single word, and put me into bed.

"I'll bring you a glass of hot milk."

"I'm sorry to be such a nuisance," I told her.

"Your aunt put my niece through college. It was supposed to be a loan, but when Gertrude made Phi Beta Kappa, Mrs. Harcourt refused any money. She just laughed and said Gertrude was a sound investment. I guess it won't hurt me any to look after you for a day or two. Or hurt you either, by the looks of you. There's nothing to worry about here. Never had a housebreaker. And that trooper says he'll sit outside your room all night. I said all right, but if he smokes, he's to use an ashtray."

How, I wondered, could I be expected to sleep after the horror of that day? Mrs. Keller, the housekeeper, had left the window half open. The cold wind blew across my eyelids and I shut my eyes. I slept.

It was half-past ten next morning when there was a tap on the door and Mrs. Keller came in with a tray. There was fruit juice and oatmeal with heavy cream and hot biscuits with butter and coffee.

"You get outside of that," she said, "and you'll be ready for anything." When she had settled the tray across my lap, she sat down and looked me over. "Well, you look some better. Had a bad time of it, haven't you? And I guess it's not over yet."

I nearly spilled the coffee. "Has something else happened?"

"Oh, no! Lands, no. I didn't mean to worry you. A trooper came to bring you some toothpaste and mouthwash and a lipstick and cold cream and I don't know what all. Said his wife had picked out the stuff. Captain Grieg called. He'd like to see you after lunch at the barracks. He'll send a car for you if you haven't transportation. Mr. Mattheson called. He'll call again. I wasn't to wake you. He asked what he could do and I said he could get rid of those reporters. Can't so much as look out of the window but there's a fellow with a camera."

I groaned.

"That's all right. A lawyer's supposed to keep folks out of trouble, isn't he? I just sent the whole lot of them over to his house. Down in the next block. The cars are lined up practically all the way to the top of the Green, but they're being made to move now, because it's almost time for church and the space will be needed."

"But you'll want to go to church," I said, noticing her black silk dress and neat black hat, the gloves and handbag she had put down beside her chair.

"Well, if you're sure you'll be all right. There's another trooper came to take the place of the one last night. The one who brought you the toothpaste and stuff. He's downstairs right now."

"You go ahead," I said, "unless Dr. Graves needs you."

"Doctor said I could go. He's out on an emergency. Said to tell you how welcome you are, but he couldn't stay. Never knew that Manning woman to have a baby at a convenient time. Five of them, counting this one.

Always come in the middle of a snowstorm, or when Doctor's car has broken down, or when he's about to take off a couple of hours for a change, or at three in the morning. Every time."

I laughed. "I suppose she can't help it." I looked down in surprise to discover that I had cleared away that breakfast without leaving a crumb.

When the housekeeper had gone, I bathed and dressed, putting on the new wool dress and rejoicing in its warmth. I had a bad moment before I could force myself to clean my teeth, but the paste had been brought by the police, so it must be safe.

The trooper, who was sitting in the living room with most of the Sunday edition of *The New York Times* scattered around him on the floor, started to get up.

When we had exchanged greetings, I asked, "Is there anything about us in the paper?"

There was a whole column in the second section, a surprisingly detailed and factual account of what had happened at the Old Mill, climaxed, of course, by the discovery last evening of Nell Glenn's body. Murder or suicide?

The newspapers from the surrounding towns were a different matter. There were headlines and pictures. The mill was referred to as the Haunted House. Starting way back when the drunken miller had killed his wife, there had been six violent deaths. The last death was under investigation. There was said to be a suicide note and confession, which the police had refused to release to the press.

When the telephone rang the trooper answered it. "You want to talk to Kendrick Knight?"

"Oh, yes."

"Good morning," Ken said. "Everything all right?"

"All right! Don't you know about Nell?"

"Good God, the whole world knows about Nell by now. By tomorrow this is going to be the biggest story in the country. And some bright newsman in Pennsylvania discovered the link between Cooper and you and the mill. A story came over the wires not an hour ago about Nell's death being the second cyanide poisoning. I wish to God—"

"What?"

"Can you get out of there without having half the reporters in the country on your trail?"

"Yes, Arthur pulled them off temporarily. He has them down at his house, giving them a story. There's no one here but the trooper who answered the phone."

"I can handle that. Suppose I pick you up in—oh, say ten minutes. Go through the house, out the back door, and cut across that vacant lot. I'll meet you on the next street."

"All right."

When the phone rang again, the trooper listened and said "Okay." He turned to me, frowning. "I'm wanted at the barracks. Will you be all right here?"

"Of course."

"Keep the doors locked and don't let anyone in," he cautioned me, "even if it's someone you know." He went out with a final doubting look, but his not to reason why.

As soon as he had gone, I got my coat, slipped out the back door, and made my way along a worn path through a vacant lot to the next street. As I emerged onto the sidewalk, Ken drew up beside me.

"Hop in."

When I got in, he turned at the nearest driveway,

backed into the road, and headed out of town. "There's no one in Vermont who wouldn't recognize you at this point," he said, "and I want to talk to you in peace."

"How did you manage about the trooper?"

"Called and said he was wanted at the barracks."

"Won't that get you in trouble?"

"I'm already in trouble."

For a while I sat quietly beside him, content not to say anything. When words came, they were going to be irrevocable, I knew that. The end wasn't far off, but there was at least this moment of peace.

"Tell me about it," he said at last, and I told him everything that had happened from the time I had got into Arthur's car until the trooper had taken me to Dr. Graves' house.

"So Maine is positive the suicide note is a fake," he said when I had finished.

"Well, she wrote, *'Sauve qui peut,'* and Maine says she didn't know a word of French."

"I remember taking her to a French restaurant once and she couldn't cope with the menu."

"But who could have got the note into her room?"

"That's obvious. It should be clear to you now."

"I hate men who try to flaunt their superior intelligence."

"I'm not flaunting anything. But you should see it."

"You know who killed them," I said.

"I think so."

"So does Maine. But why, Ken? What's behind all this? Why did so many people have to die?"

"That," he said, "is what we are going to find out."

"How can we do what the police have failed to do?"

"Because we're going to look where they didn't

think of looking. Or where they haven't looked yet. They've been busy clearing up loose ends."

"Like what?"

"Like alibis. There isn't a single alibi, of course, for the time when your aunt was killed. And when we come to her funeral, when Cooper got his, there isn't an alibi either. Nell lied when she said she and her father were together. He got out of the car at a stop-light and went to a bar. Nell picked him up there after she left the cemetery. Man in the bar told Grieg."

"And Sonia?"

Ken looked at me quickly. "You're beginning to see it, aren't you?"

"I've been pretty sure ever since I let Arthur take me home."

"What made you do that, Cathy?"

"I had a horrible minute in the dress shop." I told him what I had overheard. "It sounded so awful—"

"As though you and I were Bonnie and Clyde on a killing binge. You had to run away from the whole business."

I swallowed and then I managed a kind of grin. "I suppose that's it. I felt—unclean, as though I'd been—pawed over. I can't make you understand."

"I had that experience two years ago. I know what it's like. And then?"

"Then Arthur told me that—your wife was going to divorce you to marry him and you—stopped her, killed her. So then I knew."

"How did you know?" Ken's voice was still quiet, uninflected. But he had asked. He had a right to know.

"It came down to which of you I could believe, which of you I could trust. So I knew Arthur was lying." To forestall anything he might have to say, I

183

added hastily, "What I don't know, what I can't understand at all is how that suicide note got into Nell's room. And Cooper's billfold. And my letters."

"Sometimes, my lovely Cathy, you don't act very bright. It's one of the oldest tricks in the book. Arthur Mattheson took them in with him when he broke down that door."

16

"From the very beginning," Ken said, and his voice was like that of a stranger, "I knew that Mattheson had started making love to my wife as soon as he discovered that she was a rich woman. I don't mean that Grace was not lovable or desirable, but that wouldn't weigh with a man like Mattheson. He wanted money, and he swept her off her feet."

Because of her intense shyness and diffidence, she had known few men except for Ken, so the lawyer's tremendous vitality, his assurances that he loved her, dazzled her completely. At length he urged her to get a Reno divorce and marry him.

"He bargained," Ken went on flatly, "without two factors: Grace was very religious and she couldn't bear to hurt me. She tried—I can see that now—to tell me what had happened, but she couldn't face me with it. I suppose she was so deeply in love with him she couldn't endure living without him, but she thought it wrong to divorce me and marry him. So she threw herself in the millstream. I knew why she had done it; Mattheson knew why. It has been between us for two years.

"He has always known that I wouldn't trust him an inch, though God knows I'd have given Grace her freedom if she had asked for it. And he hates me because he tried to steal my wife. He's vain, like most criminals, and he can't forgive me for seeing him as the fortune hunter he is.

"Well, it was my knowledge of him that set me wondering when your aunt died. I'd got that note, purporting to come from her, asking me to check on the house. Later I realized she would never have called on me for such a task, she would have asked Leopold to do it. But naturally I went. And I found her there. I never for one moment believed her death was accidental, and I suspected that Mattheson had written the note to put me on the spot in case there should ever be any question about how she died. Literally on the spot."

"But, Ken, don't you see that's the weak spot. What did Arthur have to gain by killing Aunt Geraldine?"

"That," Ken said, "is what we are going to find out."

"Where are we going?"

"Down to Williamstown."

"Why on earth—"

"Because, according to Leopold, that is where he met and married his wife, who was cook in the boarding house where he was living."

"But I don't see—"

"I don't see either, but, in one way or another, Sonia Wenski, or Sarah Winters, or whatever she called herself, was at the heart of this thing. She held the key. She knew who the killer was."

"And Sonia is dead."

"She is dead, the poor little fool. If she had only been willing to talk—but I suppose she thought she had opened up an unending market for blackmail. She wasn't intelligent, the poor little devil."

"Then why would Arthur, who is intelligent, have confided in her, used her as a confederate?"

We crossed the Massachusetts line and drove to the lovely town of Williamstown, along the gracious avenues where the college buildings stand, into a dismal side street where, after passing a church and a neat parish house, Ken drew up before a run-down old house with peeling paint and dirty curtains at the windows.

"Do you want to come in with me or would you rather wait out here?"

"Why should I go in?"

"This is the house where Sonia was cook and Leopold a roomer."

"I'll wait for you."

"No," Ken said abruptly, "come along. I don't like the idea of leaving you alone."

The owner looked as run-down as the house and almost as dirty. She wore torn bedroom slippers, there were ladders in her stockings, her hair was in curlers vaguely covered by a net, her slip showed, her skirt was well above her knees though she must have been in the middle fifties, with heavy legs.

"You looking for a room?"

She stepped back and Ken let me go ahead of him. The smell of the place was enough to knock me out, stale smoke, stale cooking, a lingering odor of onions and cabbage.

When Ken had closed the door, he said, "We want to inquire about a former lodger of yours, Leonard Winters."

Her expression changed from an ingratiating smile to a look of profound suspicion and distrust. "You a policeman? I told the police he'd lived here and was a good quiet tenant. What more do you want?"

"I'm not a policeman." There was a ten-dollar bill in

Ken's hand and it disappeared by legerdemain into the woman's pocket.

"You a newspaperman?"

Ken nodded. After all, it was true. She brightened. "Well, now." She put a hand to the curlers. "Would you be wanting pictures? Soon as my hair dries—"

"Later, probably," Ken said, making her perfectly happy.

I couldn't see that she made anything clearer. Leonard Winters had rented a room on the top floor, small but nice, she assured me, for three months. There was a church down the street and he'd made arrangements with the minister, a nice man, real nice, to let him use the piano in the basement where Sunday school was held. He had spent most of his time in the church except when they had meetings.

"This is where he met his wife, isn't it?"

"Yeah. Sarah Mason. Only good cook I've ever had, and the saving kind, too. Most of them can't so much as peel a potato without whittling it all away. But everyone liked Sarah's cooking, and she was real dependable. Only one time she was late with a meal and that wasn't hardly her fault. She'd run out to the store for something and the minister called her in as she was passing the church. He needed another witness for a wedding."

No, she hadn't known her tenant and her cook were seeing much of each other until a week or so later, when they got married. A while after that, maybe two weeks, they moved away to that Old Mill, the one there had been so much about in the paper. Sarah was tickled pink about it, but much good it had done the poor kid. Not two months married and she gets stabbed to death by a masked man. A masked man!

Queer doings. Thinks she's hit the jackpot and all she gets is a knife in the guts.

"Did she tell you she'd hit the jackpot?" Ken asked her.

"No, she was real close-mouthed. But after she witnessed that wedding at the church, something happened; you could see she was thinking hard. Not long after there was a picture in the paper about some man, a lawyer winning a case. Good-looking man. And she said, 'It says here he's a popular bachelor whose law reputation is growing by leaps and bounds. A bachelor!' Then she wrote a letter. And the next thing I knew, she was telling me Leonard had been asked to play for a rich woman and the woman was going to stake him."

When the owner of the boarding house had finished telling us the little she knew, she went back to tell us all over again, adding comments about her own feelings at the time and saying how you never could tell the way things would turn out.

When we finally managed to get away from her and stood on the doorstep, I took a long breath of the cold, sweet, untainted air. Ken held my arm. "Come along. I don't want you out of my sight."

"Where are we going now?" I asked in surprise.

"The church next door. I want to check on that wedding for which Sarah Winters was a witness, and which made such a change in her life."

We found the minister in the rectory, tall and thin and pale and shabby. His hair and his skin were both gray in tone. He had a gentle voice that was inclined to intone what he had to say, making the banal sound important, which, I suppose, was an occupational hazard. His manner was kind, halfway between an in-

189

nate humility and the confidence that comes of being pastor of a flock.

He smiled at us. "Are you planning to be married?"

"No, sir, we came to you to discuss another wedding, one you performed two or three months ago."

"Nothing wrong, I hope."

"I hope so too, sir."

The minister's chair in the shabby rectory had a worn seat, sagging springs, and torn upholstery. There were too many small tables and plants in the room, but the place was neat enough. He opened a register on the table, looked up at Ken expectantly.

"But, first, can you tell us anything about Leonard Winters?"

"Winters? Oh, the young musician! He played rather well, I thought, certainly better than our regular organist. I let him practice on the piano in the basement where we hold meetings, and in return he offered to play the organ for church services and choir practice. Very meticulous about filling his obligations. I was sorry to have him leave. We have a schoolteacher playing for us now, but there's a difference." He shook his head. "Quite a difference."

I could imagine.

"Still," and he brightened, "I wouldn't have wanted to stand in his way when I heard of this offer, a room and piano and expenses, and even his opening recital paid for. I was very happy for him."

"Who told you about it?"

The minister beamed at us. "Wonderful, wasn't it? People are so apt to forget the goodness of God."

And of Aunt Geraldine, I thought.

"Did you know his wife?" Ken asked.

"Oh, yes. Well, at least I had seen her several times. I married them, you know. Let's see—" He hunted back in his register and looked faintly surprised when he found the entry. "Yes, here it is: Sarah Mason to Leonard Winters, August the third."

"You say you'd seen her around?"

"As you do people who live practically next door. She was a cook, I believe. And one day I called her in when only my wife was here and I needed another witness for a wedding. She was just passing the house. Providence is wonderful."

I thought of what Providence had done for Sonia and I shivered.

"Yes, yes, here it is." His finger was moving along the page. "July the twelfth. Ella Harcourt Glenn to Arthur Mattheson."

I couldn't have spoken if my life had depended on it, but there was a look of elation in Ken's narrow eyes. They practically glittered like a lion's before it springs on its prey.

When I could think at all, I heard the minister's embarrassed murmur of protest, and heard Ken say, "For your poor box." He was steering me toward the door. He turned back. "Look here, sir, if I were you, I would keep that register under lock and key for the next few days."

The minister smiled. He was probably used to the vagaries of human beings. "No one is likely to bother it. It has been here quite safely for fifteen years."

"Four people have died because of that little item in your register," Ken told him, and opened the door for me.

II

"So that was it," I said when we were outside.

"That's the way it had to be. Sonia was the one real risk that Mattheson ran. She witnessed his marriage to

Nell, by which he expected to get a third of the Harcourt estate. Then she saw his picture in the paper and the comment about his being a bachelor. She wanted Leonard, God knows why! but she needed something more than the ability to cook to catch a man like that. There was a chance that this rising young lawyer would pay to keep his marriage secret. Obviously, as soon as he heard from her, Mattheson knew what he was up against. If he went ahead with his plans to eliminate Mrs. Harcourt, there was always a chance that the girl would speak out and give away his motive. So when she wanted help for Leopold, he talked your aunt into hearing him, and Leopold was good. Better than good. At least, by having them under his eyes, Mattheson would know where he stood, and the girl would realize that she'd follow when he cracked the whip or she'd lose everything.

"I'm guessing that, in return for his arranging for Mrs. Harcourt's financial help, he got her to produce the illusory shadows that were intended to make your aunt question her own reason or provide an excuse for committing her as mentally incompetent. Whatever happened, she was promised a safe future."

"In other words, Arthur married Nell because he wanted Aunt Geraldine's money."

"He wanted it. And how. But he had to take Nell along with it—Nell who was already chasing Leopold and God knows who else. Then Sonia witnessed the second will and told him. He obviously hired Cooper to get rid of you, and Cooper—thank God!—failed. He planned your aunt's death and there he succeeded. Then he changed his plans in midstream. He took one look at you, not only the heiress but a beautiful woman and one who could be relied on for normal integrity and honor. And he was stuck with Nell."

"What do you think really happened?"

"I think Mattheson arranged to meet Cooper at the mill. He was going to involve me if he could, because I had already announced that I would not attend the services, and the chances were that I'd have no alibi."

"But if he planned to kill Cooper, why did he bring Sonia back with him?"

"God knows. I might have produced a cast-iron alibi."

"So she was to be involved in Cooper's death?"

"I suppose so. Anyhow, when she began to threaten, that was the end for her. After he killed her, he planted the mask and knife in the studio, of course."

Ken became aware that the minister had drawn aside a curtain and was watching us in some surprise, wondering why we were lingering on his doorsteps. "Just a minute. I'll call Grieg from here and put him in the picture about what we have learned. He'll want to pick up Mattheson for questioning and, for my money, the sooner the better. You wait in the car while I use the minister's telephone."

While he waited for the minister to come to the door, I went out to the car. There was another car parked behind it and, to my relief, I noticed the trooper's broad hat. I went up to the car and the driver signaled for me to get in. I did so.

The motor had been running and the car moved away from the curb. "Don't try to jump, Cathy," Arthur Mattheson said. "You'd break one of those pretty legs. And that would be a pity."

17

"Where are you taking me?" I asked when I had caught my breath.

"Where we'll be safe until I can do some fresh planning."

"There isn't any such place," I told him. "Ken knows. He's calling Captain Grieg now."

Arthur smiled. "No, whatever he is doing, Knight is not taking Captain Grieg into his confidence."

"You sound very sure."

"He looked out of the window and saw us take off. He has sense enough to know that you will be safe only as long as I am."

We had left Williamstown behind and we were heading north toward Bennington on Route Seven. I wondered whether Arthur was going to try to make the Canadian border. There wasn't, so far as I could see, anything else he could do, but if he stuck to the major highway, he'd never make it.

He was intent on his thoughts, and I stole a look at him. He didn't seem to be greatly worried, just thoughtful. He was weighing pros and cons coolly. I looked at the door, trying to remember how the thing opened, so that if I had a chance I wouldn't fumble.

"I have a revolver," Arthur said without bothering to turn his head. "There's small chance you could jump at the speed we are traveling without serious injury—painful injury. And if you did manage to get out, I wouldn't hesitate to shoot. I have nothing to lose from one more murder, you know."

"What do you have to gain?"

"Time. Knight won't call the police. He won't dare. He knows if he ever wants to see you again, he has got to keep his damned hands off."

"What chance has he of seeing me again? Alive, I mean."

"That depends on you, my dear. But I warn you, Cathy, don't try to call for help when we drive through Bennington. I promise you that would be the last sound you would ever make."

"I believe you really like killing."

"You are wrong. The only person I have ever longed to kill is Kendrick Knight. But maybe I can hurt him worse this way."

Nothing he could have said would have sealed my fate so completely. He would enjoy killing me because of the pain it would inflict on Ken. Even if the police were, incredibly and impossibly, to offer him complete freedom for releasing me, Arthur wouldn't do it. His hatred was deeper even than his sense of self-preservation.

Sooner or later, perhaps in minutes, perhaps in hours, Arthur was going to kill me. I didn't doubt it, but I didn't believe it. I wonder whether anyone really believes he is going to die. It is practically impossible to imagine life going on in a world where you don't exist. I wonder whether even people condemned to the electric chair or the gas chamber or to being hanged believe that it can happen, even at the last minute. Surely something will intervene—something will stop the insupportable.

I wondered dimly how Arthur planned to kill me; he

had thrown Aunt Geraldine down the stairs so she had broken her neck; he had struck Tim Cooper on the head and thrown him into the millstream; he had stabbed Sonia; he had poisoned Nell, his wife. Would he shoot me? I hoped, at least, it would be quick.

What was Ken doing? His hands were tied unless he let Arthur kill me. Or did he realize it wouldn't matter one way or another what he did? No one knew better or understood better the depth of Arthur's hatred for him and the lengths to which it could drive him. It was the one thing—that corroding hatred—they had in common.

From the beginning, Ken had blocked Arthur. His poor wife had preferred to kill herself rather than run away with Arthur, though she loved him, and Arthur had lost her fortune, which had gone to Ken. Ken had helped Aunt Geraldine with the second will, which disinherited Nell whom Arthur had married, and so another fortune had been wrested from his hands. Ken had unearthed the fatal link between Sonia and Arthur. He had, within the past hour, discovered the secret marriage to Nell, which was to have been Arthur's triumph when the proper time came and was now his defeat. And, though I knew it didn't count much with a man like Arthur, Ken had my love—if he wanted it— and Arthur had failed with me, too.

"What do you really expect now?" I asked at last.

"I've got to get back to the drawing board. If Knight cares a rap about you, he'll give me that time."

"But Ken isn't the only one who knows."

Arthur chuckled. "You aren't a very good liar, are you?"

"Do you honestly think you can get away with five murders—counting me?"

196

"Mrs. Harcourt fell down the stairs," Arthur told me blandly. "We have the evidence of the medical examiner who was also her devoted friend, and who is highly regarded in the community. Tim Cooper died while I was at your aunt's funeral. His missing papers were found in Nell's room. Sonia was stabbed by a masked man whom no one could identify, a man who disappeared afterwards. The knife and mask were found in her husband's room. And poor Nell"— hearing the mockery in his voice, I began to understand what hate means—"chose an unusual way in which to commit suicide, after leaving a confession."

"Too bad you slipped up about her knowing French," I said, and then caught my breath as I saw his expression. If I wanted to buy time, any time at all, I had better be careful. A word, a gesture, would set him off. If I had been walking a tight rope for the past few days, with no net below, Arthur was balancing out over an abyss. At that moment he was as dangerous as a coiled rattlesnake, and I knew it.

He was trained in the law. If he simply kept still and denied everything—except his marriage, of course— he stood a good chance of going free. He balanced on a razor's edge between self-preservation and a driving, irrational need to give hatred its way.

"Guthrie is a lush," he said abruptly. "Give him enough free liquor and his living and he'd never make trouble. Maine is a pleasant weakling, not interested in money or anything but his rather precious writing, until he fell for you. His only worry was Nell and trying to keep her out of trouble. He'd have welcomed our marriage because it passed on the responsibility for her to me; Nell would have been as easy to handle as cutting into a poached egg. Just give her enough rope.

And I didn't care whether she chased every man in the village, as long as she stayed married to me. If there should be too much scandal about her carrying-on, we could always move on somewhere else. On all that money. It was all cut and dried.

"And then you showed up. You take the jackpot. And Ken, apparently, takes you. Or thought he was going to."

"Arthur!" It was degrading, but I had no pride left. I was begging for my life. "Arthur, please let me go. Please! Please! There's no proof against you. Please!"

"And give you to Ken?"

"What difference would it make? He doesn't even want me, so far as I know. And you don't. Not really."

As we reached Bennington, he reached out and gripped my arm so tightly he hurt me. "Cathy, let's have no misunderstanding. It would be a fatal mistake if you did anything to attract attention. Wave or call out or anything like that. Fatal. Do you understand?"

I had said all I could. I tried to speak but my mouth was dry. I couldn't even manage to swallow. I nodded my head.

"Yes, I see you do. Be a good girl. A sensible girl."

There were people on the streets as we went through Bennington, people in cars, a patrol car, a traffic policeman at a light where Route Seven crosses the Molly Stark Trail at Number Nine. It would have been so easy to shout, to wave, to do something. But Arthur drove with his left hand and his right held the revolver, a man so possessed by hatred that reason was suspended.

We passed the business section, the roadside stands, the motels on the highway. It was country again—the lovely rolling peaceful country of Vermont.

And suddenly I knew. "Why, we're going back to the Old Mill!"

After all, it was the logical place. The police had ordered everyone out. No one would expect Arthur to bring me here, even if the police knew Arthur had me. What had Ken decided to do? Was he gambling on telling the police? Would he try to find me himself? Would he wait for Arthur's next move? But he must know as well as I knew that when Arthur had followed us to Williamstown and guessed that we knew of his marriage, which provided the motive for the murders, he would hold me hostage until Ken assured him that he would be safe.

Unexpectedly he braked, backed, and then turned off the road. There was a narrow dirt lane on the right and he followed it, driving slowly over ruts, to an abandoned farm with a ramshackle barn that had been converted into a garage. Arthur got out to open the door of the garage. I put my hand on the car door and let it drop again. How far could I run before a bullet stopped me? While I obeyed him, I was still alive.

He drove the car in and shut off the motor. "All right. Get out."

For a moment I felt that I could not move. Was this the last stop for me? This abandoned farm? I might lie here for weeks, months, before my body was discovered, before Ken knew what had happened to me. Then I got out, stumbling a little, my knees so weak they barely held me up.

As I reached the garage door, Arthur said, "Wait! People have seen that coat of yours." Off the floor in the back of the car he pulled a shabby old raincoat, which must have been short for him but was long for me, even when pulled over my own coat.

He groped around for an old cap and pulled it over my hair. It was dirty and smelled of oil; evidently he had worn it when doing some mechanical work on the car.

"I guess that's all right. No, wait!" He went back to rummage in the glove compartment for dark glasses, which he shoved on my nose.

"We're going to keep off Main Street when we get into Milltown. You are going to walk quietly. No funny stuff. Understand?" Arthur laughed as he saw my expression. "I see you do."

I had thought Milltown was practically a one-street town until I accompanied Arthur through a maze of narrow streets that had a disconcerting habit of going steeply downhill. They weren't pretty streets. Arthur was alert, watching people in cars and on the street, watching windows for anyone who might be looking out, as wary as a cat.

The afternoon was getting raw, and a sharp wind swirled dead leaves around our feet with a whispering sound. Then Arthur gripped my arm more tightly. This was the dangerous moment when he must cross Main Street. We did so in a rush and then we were on the winding lane that led to the Old Mill. Only when we had rounded a curve and were out of sight of the village did he relax, but he kept that steel grip on my arm.

The closer we got to the mill, the more clearly I remembered every detail of what had happened there. I gave a sudden exclamation.

"What's that?" Arthur demanded sharply. "See anyone?" His nerves were on edge, too, for all his air of confidence. He must be looking into the abyss beneath his feet. One false step—

"No, I didn't see anyone. I just realized that Nell

knew you were guilty. That's why she had hysterics. She knew and she was afraid."

"She should have known I could take care of myself."

"What an egoist you are! Not afraid for you. Afraid of you."

We had come to the rustic bridge now. Arthur stood there for a long time scanning the windows of the house and listening. I listened, too, but all I could hear was the noisy chatter of the brook and the rustle of dead autumn leaves stirred by the wind. It seemed to me that a curtain at the window in my room moved, but I remembered that the window had been opened a little bit.

"How did you get that cyanide into Nell's toothpaste?" I asked.

"She always used the same brand," Arthur said almost indifferently. "I replaced the tube several days ago. I didn't know when she'd work down to the poison."

"And you didn't care."

"As you say. By that time I had my eye on you. You have a fairly lethal effect on men, Cathy."

"I hope so," I said through set teeth.

Arthur laughed. "You've got a lot of spirit, haven't you? God, what a pair we could have made, Cathy. Your beauty and quality and—"

"And money. You wouldn't want a girl who couldn't keep you."

That was a mistake. I knew it before he moved. Then he slapped me across the face so hard that he knocked me off balance and I nearly fell. There was something in his eyes I had never seen before, but I knew it had been there: when Aunt Geraldine hurtled down the stairs; when Tim Cooper plunged into the millstream; when Sonia was stabbed; when cyanide was forced into the tube of toothpaste. It wasn't just the money, I realized then. Arthur was one of life's mavericks, a born rogue. A born killer. He liked it.

On the side porch he fumbled in the cloisonné vase for the key, cursed, and tried the door, which opened under his hand.

The heat had been turned down and the mill was chilly, as it had been when I arrived—how long ago? Arthur went to turn up the thermostat, and the furnace thumped as it came on.

"I'd like to wash," I said.

He shook his head. "Sorry, you aren't going to lock yourself in a bathroom."

"What am I going to do?"

Arthur went into the dining room to pour himself a drink and, as an afterthought, he brought me one, too, a light Scotch and soda. When he had refilled his own glass, he dropped into a chair near me and I realized for the first time, and without any pity, that he was almost exhausted. His skin seemed slack around his jaw, his eyes were sunken in his head, there were new lines around his mouth. He vibrated like a violin string. I wondered when he had last slept and whether he had dreamed. Even a born killer must dream sometimes.

From somewhere he drew on a fresh reserve of energy. He got up. "Come on."

I gripped the arms of the chair and my heart was pounding like drums in some African festival.

"Come on," he said impatiently. "Food. We've got to have food. It's nearly five o'clock."

In the kitchen, while he sat on a bar stool against the wall, the revolver dangling loosely in his hand, I made turkey sandwiches, put on coffee, and sliced what was left of the pumpkin pie.

Oddly enough, I ate hungrily. The condemned man may not always eat a hearty meal, but I did, and when I had finished, I felt better. Courage seemed to flow back and even, like a distant spark, somewhere, hope. Which was absurd. I was afraid to encourage it.

The food and the coffee had helped Arthur, too. He pushed back from the table, his face alight.

"Well, I'll be damned," he said. "I will be eternally damned."

"I certainly hope so," I said cordially.

"I must have needed rest. That's why I was so slow to see it."

"See what?"

"Knight. The Patsy. The stooge. He's a natural. You see it, Cathy my sweet? Kendrick Knight sneaked you out from under the eyes of the trooper Grieg had looking after you. Kendrick Knight killed his wife for her money; he found Mrs. Harcourt's body; he found Tim Cooper's body; he arranged that second will. He appeared on the scene just before poor little Sonia was knifed. He was one of Nell's infatuations. He wanted you—how he wanted you!—after you inherited. And Kendrick Knight, my sweet and fiery love, has his hands tied. A word from him and he loses you. What a sweet setup, and it took me all this time to think of it. I must be slipping."

"Anyone could have told you that." I picked up the coffeepot and hurled it at him, the boiling water streaming over his head and down his face. I heard him yell with pain as I kicked the revolver across the room and ran for the door.

I was through the kitchen, the dining room, and across the porch before Arthur got into action. I didn't know how much damage the boiling water had done, but I hoped fervently that it was hurting like hell. I was afraid of the house and instinctively sought the out of doors.

It was nearly dark. The ground had lost its faded purples and reds and golds, and now it was only a monochrome of rustling darkness. The sky was still light toward the west, but the lawn and the gardens were filled with shadows as the house had seemed to be. The dry leaves rustled as though small animals were moving through them.

I started toward the driveway and then Arthur was after me, running hard, faster than I possibly could, with his longer stride and greater endurance. I swerved toward the woods, where there were some big trees, primary growth, with huge trunks. Somewhere in the dusk I could hide. Somewhere I could escape those pounding feet.

Then he stepped out almost in front of me—how had he got there?—and I swerved with a scream, high and despairing, toward the millstream. It was almost as though I had always known that this was where it would all have to end.

Someone shouted "Cathy!"

I put on a burst of speed, tripped over a rock half hidden in fallen leaves, regained my balance, plunged on. My breath was rasping in my throat now. My heart felt like a hammer, breaking through my side. I couldn't go on like this.

There was a flash and a report, and a twig dropped off the tree in front of me, fell to the ground. Again I slipped. Arthur had found his revolver. No matter how fast I ran, I couldn't outrun the speed of a bullet.

I stopped short, turned abruptly. Anything was better than this. All I wanted was to end that hideous flight, that shameful attempt to prolong my life by one more minute.

"All right," I said. "All right." Under me my foot slipped on wet autumn leaves. My arms thrashed. Two guns went off, almost at the same time, and I fell. The last thing I remember was the loud rush of the mill-stream. Then the water was over my face.

18

"Of course," Ken said infuriatingly, "you were never in any real danger. From the moment Mattheson took off with you, the police in Massachusetts and Vermont were alerted. Unmarked cars never lost sight of you. The mill had half a dozen people hidden all around the place before you ever got there."

I'd been kidnaped and scared out of my wits and slapped and threatened and shot at. For about ten seconds I'd thought I was being killed. In movies they do these things better. There would have been a thrilling scene of my late-minute rescue from the killer and a fade-out in the arms of the hero.

Hero, huh!

Ken was sitting beside my bed in Dr. Graves's house. There was nothing improper about that, heavens knows. Half of Milltown seemed to be there, at least the uniformed force.

Ken had fished me out of the millstream, dripping like a discarded scrubcloth, and he had driven me, hell bent for leather, to the doctor's house, where Mrs. Keller once more undressed me and put me to bed. The doctor had looked me over and decided that I would live and ordered everyone out. Everyone meant Ken and Captain Grieg and Sergeant Mendelssohn and Maine Harcourt, who had come from the motel when he heard the news.

"All you need is a night's sleep," Dr. Graves assured me.

"Sleep!" I wailed. "I can't sleep until I know what happened."

He gave me the patient smile doctors save for unreasonable patients, and held a glass at my lips. "Drink this," he said, like something in Alice in Wonderland.

And then it was the next day and no reason on earth why I should not get up except that people arrived in hordes before there was time to dress.

I had told my story over and over and then Ken had said smugly, "Of course, you were never in any real danger."

If I hadn't seen his knuckles turn white as he gripped the quilt, I'd have been tempted to throw something at him.

"I guess," Captain Grieg said, standing up, "that pretty well wraps it up."

"Isn't anyone going to tell me what happened?"

Grieg laughed. "You have that coming to you, I think."

"Don't give me too much credit; it might go to my head. All I did was bring you a murderer all wrapped up in cellophane."

"You did at that. Not often we catch a guy red-handed."

"You did catch him?" For a moment, last night's terror had me by the throat. Ken reached up and caught my hand in his.

"That was Sergeant Mendelssohn. Very pretty shooting. Shot his revolver out of his hand. You needn't worry about Mattheson, Miss Briggs. We've got him locked up and where he's going, he won't bother anyone for a long, long time. If we didn't have anything but his attempt to kill you—and five witnesses!—we'd have him in more trouble than he'll know now to cope with."

"Were you very much surprised?" I asked.

Grieg hesitated. "Knight's been at us ever since your aunt's death, but there was no motive we could see—until we found out about his marriage, of course." Grieg glanced awkwardly at Maine, who had been leaning against the door.

"I began to think it was Arthur when Nell went to pieces that way. I knew she was involved somehow and he seemed to be the only possible—" Maine broke off. "The Harcourts haven't done much to make you like them, have they, Cathy? I did try—"

"I know you did."

"Well," he pushed away from the door, "I'd like to see you, say good-by before Dad and I push off. We won't be leaving until after the inquests, of course, and we won't go far. We'll have to come back for the trial. Will you be here?"

"I don't know."

Maine started a general exodus. He was followed by Captain Grieg and Sergeant Mendelssohn and two men in uniform whose names I didn't know.

Mrs. Keller, who had been hovering outside the bedroom door, came charging in. She waited, arms folded, her eyes on Ken, who got up quickly.

"Time Miss Briggs had a chance to bathe and dress," Mrs. Keller said austerely.

Ken gave me a curt nod. "I've got to get to work. I have a paper to get out and the biggest story we've ever handled to write."

"Will I see you later?"

"Not today. Probably I'll be on the job all night."

I looked after him rather blankly and then I bathed and dressed. When Dr. Graves had completed his hospital rounds and came home for lunch, we had a long talk. Not about the horrors that lay behind, about what lay ahead. He arranged to find me another lawyer.

"Are you planning to stay here?" Dr. Graves asked.

I nodded. "That's what Aunt Geraldine wanted. Anyhow, I think it would be great fun to create an art colony, if I can find advisers to help with the project. And first I want to do something about Maine and his father. That is, as soon as the estate is clear."

"Old Harcourt isn't to be trusted with money."

"I realize that, but Maine is. Certainly something can be done to provide him with a moderate income, so he can write what he likes without pressure and still be able to look after his father. And I want to carry out Aunt Geraldine's wishes in regard to Leopold."

"How about the mill?" the doctor asked. "Will you mind staying there, with all the violence and tragedy that have occurred in the place?"

"I don't know," I admitted.

"At least, you'll stay here, won't you, until things are settled. You won't go to the mill alone?"

"No, I won't go to the mill alone."

The rest of that day I spent avoiding the door and the telephone, afraid even to look out of a window because the place was besieged with reporters and cameramen and the curious. Ken didn't come or telephone.

Next day, Captain Grieg called to say that people were overrunning the grounds of the Old Mill. He was stationing a trooper for the day, but he didn't have extra men for jobs of that kind. Did I want to hire a watchman?

"What about Leopold?" I suggested. "He can watch the house and at the same time have an opportunity to practice to his heart's content."

"Do you trust that guy?"

"Well, he wouldn't let anything interfere with his music. Yes, I'm willing to trust him."

Maine had left the Cadillac at the doctor's house for me. He hadn't made any further attempt to see me, for which I was grateful. By the end of another day the reporters and the sightseers had withdrawn, looking for more likely quarry, and I was preparing to go to the Old Mill, pick up the rest of my things, and arrange with Leopold about some sort of salary, his food, and incidentals, until the will was settled.

The weather had changed. It was a gray November day, the hills barren of foliage, a hint of snow in the air, when I finally got under the wheel of the big car and sat looking at the unfamiliar dashboard.

Ken stood beside the driver's seat. "Lady, can you give me a lift?"

I moved over in relief. "Drive, will you, until I get used to this thing? It feels like a locomotive. I'm used to a Volkswagen."

He slid in beside me. He didn't seem to be in a talkative mood.

"Did you get your story written?" I asked at last.

He nodded. "Brought you a copy. Something for you to remember when you get back home."

"When I—" I swallowed. "I was planning to stay on here, Ken."

He started the car. "Where to?"

"The mill. I want to get some things and talk to Leopold."

"What's he doing there?"

"Acting as watchman to keep off sightseers, and practicing."

"You can't very well stay at the mill with Leopold."

210

"Oh, Dr. Graves has asked me to stay at his house until I can get someone to stay at the mill with me, and the estate is settled."

"Look here, Cathy, why don't you get the hell back home? You have a normal life of your own there. The mill has become a place of horrors. Anyhow, it's too big for you. And you're going to be a very rich woman. You can do what you like with your life from now on."

"But Aunt Geraldine—"

"No one would dream of making you hold to the terms she suggested in her will, not after what has happened at the mill."

"It had a bad reputation when Aunt Geraldine bought it and made it beautiful. If I go ahead with the art colony, that should help counteract the destructive things, make the place all alive with what's creative."

Ken was turning into the driveway. "So you're determined to stay here." He was markedly without enthusiasm.

He shut off the motor. From the studio I could hear Leopold playing "Sheep May Safely Graze."

"That's what I mean," I said.

"You'll need a staff."

"It shouldn't be hard to get one."

"With the reputation this place has?"

"I wish you wouldn't be such an obstructionist!"

"You don't know what you're attempting, Cathy." Ken still had not turned to look at me. He sat staring at the mill as though he had never seen it before. "You'll need a good lawyer and someone to handle money. You can't expect to cope with that yourself."

"I don't. I know I'll need help."

"And you'll need an adviser to help set up the foundation Mrs. Harcourt had in mind."

"I'd been hoping that you would advise me about things, Ken."

"Not me," he said quickly. "Sorry, Cathy, but that's out. I don't intend to have any hand in the management of the Harcourt money."

"Well, that seems to be that." I opened the door and got out.

"You're damned right. Never again can anyone say I want any part in any woman's money."

I fitted the key Captain Grieg had given me into the lock and went into the big living room. As I might have expected, it was cold. I turned up the thermostat. In the studio Leopold was playing something modern and dissonant.

"A hell of a watchdog he's going to be," Ken remarked. He was in a foul humor and I didn't know what to do about it. In the circumstances I thought I'd try shock tactics.

"Ken, if it weren't for Aunt Geraldine's money, would you still want me to go away?"

Shock was right. He pulled out a pipe and took his time filling and lighting it. Then he said, "You must know, damned well, that with your looks you could get anyone you wanted whether you had a cent or not."

"Apparently not," I told him. "Look, you dope, do I have to—"

Ken's sort of esthetic-looking. I wouldn't have believed it.

"Hey," I protested at last, not very wholeheartedly but because I had to breathe.

"I suppose you know," he told me, "that everyone will think I'm a fortune hunter."

"Of course," I agreed, "though it's not very complimentary to me."

He reached for me again and then stood back, shaking his head. "You are dynamite," he told me. "I don't dare spend any more time dallying with you, young woman. I'm taking you back to Dr. Graves. If we don't go now, we won't go at all."

"That suits me," I said contentedly.

"I have my reputation to consider," Ken said. He kissed me hard—once. Then he called to Leopold, "Look after the joint," and he took me out to the car.